THE ENDURING FLAME

Inside his log cabin, in the Great White Wilderness, young Joanna Grey's father dies, and she's forced to flee from the lecherous Conrad Owen into the icy wilderness. Lost and exhausted, she's found by Richard Strange and they shelter in a cabin where they become trapped by raging snowstorms. And, despite discovering their love for one another, they agree that John should return to his wife. But then, terrifyingly for Joanna alone in the arctic night, Conrad Owen appears . . .

DENISE ROBINS

THE ENDURING FLAME

Complete and Unabridged

LINFORD
Leicester

First published in Great Britain in 1929

First Linford Edition
published 2010

British Library CIP Data

Robins, Denise, *1897 –1985*.
    The enduring flame.- -
    (Linford romance library)
    1. Love stories. 2. Large type books.
    I. Title II. Series
    823.9'12–dc22

    ISBN 978–1–44480–074–6

Published by
F. A. Thorpe (Publishing)
Anstey, Leicestershire

Set by Words & Graphics Ltd.
Anstey, Leicestershire
Printed and bound in Great Britain by
T. J. International Ltd., Padstow, Cornwall

This book is printed on acid-free paper

1

Snow was beginning to fall again.

Great white flakes, greyish in the dimming light of early afternoon, whirled and spat against the window pane of John Grey's log-cabin in the Great White Wilderness. The wind howled furiously down the chimney and moaned like a lost spirit round the cabin. But John Grey heard nothing, saw nothing. Still and pallid he lay on his camp bed in the living room, drawn up close to the fire. It shed a red glow upon him, but even in that glow he was marble-white. Rigid features, a calm, bearded face, long rough hair, hands of skeleton thinness lying outside the coverlet.

John Grey was dead.

Beside him crouched a girl. She might have been a boy . . . slender, lithe little figure in breeches, leggings, fur

1

coat. Small cropped head covered with dark, crisp curls. Boyish hands, brown, used to rough work. Only the face was purely girl, oval, chiselled, with great dark long-lashed eyes and a small mouth. Fire and passion and endurance in every line of Joanna Grey's face. She had learned endurance out here on the Yukon for the last twelve years. She had been through the bitter struggles which men face in the Gold Rush. She had shared hunger, pain, privation, failure, with her father. From the age of five she had lived out here in the snows with him and their Indian servant. She had known no other home, no women friends. Only men . . . some who were kind, some from whom she had learned to protect herself. She had cared for nobody but her father.

And now he was dead.

Jo — he had always called her that — had watched him die at dawn. She had sat like this ever since, watching her dead, dumbly suffering, brooding.

She was appalled to find herself

2

alone, without Daddy. She was bewildered because she did not know where to go or what to do. But she tried not to be afraid. She had no fear of Death. She had seen so many men die, of cold, of fever, of starvation. Daddy's still, silent form did not horrify her. It only filled her with speechless grief. It was Life she feared . . . Life in the form of many rough strange men who trail through the White Wilderness. She wished, passionately, that she had been a boy. But she was a girl of eighteen. She wondered where to go and what would happen to her.

Outside, Kiche, which means Wolf, the Indian servant who had loved her father and who was her slave, had gone with his team of Eskimo dogs to fetch a coffin and a priest to give John Grey Christian burial. She felt very hungry and lonely. Her firm little mouth turned down at the corners. She hid her face in her hands. But she could not cry.

Then in a swift startled way she sprang to her feet, every nerve jumping, eyes large and bright. She sprang to the door and reached out for her rifle. There came the sound of a man's voice.

'Hi, you, Jo. Are you there? Let me in.'

Her arms dropped to her sides. The colour receded from her face. It was Conrad Owen, a fur-trader who had known her father. Several times she had seen him and talked to him over a mug of coffee. She did not like him. There was a certain secret look in his eyes that she only half understood but disliked. But now that her father was dead and the terrible sense of loneliness was crushing her she felt she would be glad to talk to even the fur-trader.

She unbarred the door and let him in.

Conrad Owen entered, stamping the snow from his boots and blowing on his hands.

'Good evening to you, Jo,' he said.

She did not answer, but pointed mutely to the still body of John Grey under his fur rug. Conrad Owen uttered a low whistle and walked up to the bed. Then he turned to the girl.

'Yes. He died at dawn,' she said. 'You knew he was ill when you last passed our way.'

'Sure, I knew that. But I'm sorry he's gone.'

'Yes,' said Joanna. Her voice quivered with pain. The man looked at her while he unbuttoned his bearskin coat and took off his round fur cap. He looked at her curiously. A strange, wild little thing, Joanna Grey. He admired her spirit. More than that. He wanted her beauty, the redness of her lips and the soft pale curve of her throat. There was no girl like this for miles around . . . none so soft, so pretty, so virginal and at the same time so untamed and fierce.

And old Grey was dead and the girl was alone. That was news. He walked up to her, thumbs in the lapels of his leather jacket.

'What you going to do, kid?' he asked.

'I don't know,' she said wearily.

'You got no relations?'

'None that I know.'

'Where'd he come from?'

'London.'

'Why'd he come out to the Yukon? For gold?'

She resented the cross-examination. She answered reluctantly:

'I don't know much about it.'

That was true. She knew so little. John Grey had never told her very much about his past. She only knew that when she had been a baby of five her mother had died and he, at that period of his life, drinking heavily, had because of some shameful deed, something connected with forging a cheque, left England forever.

He had brought her out to the Yukon. For all these years they had been everything to each other. He had made gold and lost it again. Now illness had overtaken him and death put an end to the striving. He had died as he had lived, a failure. Poor, lovable, weak John

6

Grey. And he had left her, his Jo, with nothing in the world, he who would have given her everything.

She moved away from Conrad Owen.

'I shall go to Fort Yukon later when my father is buried,' she said brusquely.

Conrad Owen passed a forefinger over his lips. He stood watching her, thinking. He was a handsome man in his fashion, huge, muscular. But coarse and florid. Yellow hair and china-blue eyes gave him a Germanic appearance. He had a loose mouth and that way of looking at her which caused her uneasiness.

She walked into the adjoining room which was a kind of kitchenette and where she slept, herself.

'You would like food and coffee,' she said.

He followed her.

'Jo,' he said. 'Look here. No need for you to be all alone, kid. No need to trail to Fort Yukon by yourself. You come along o' me.'

'No thanks, Conrad,' she said.

'Sure, why not?'

'I'd rather be by myself. I shall get work.'

'Work — you — a baby!' he jeered.

She swung round.

'I am no baby. I can take care of myself.'

'A woman, then ... the chaps will rush for you.'

'Let them rush. I can take care of myself,' she repeated with fierce pride.

Conrad Owen rubbed his hands together. He gave a little, low chuckle. John Grey lay dead in the next room. Little Jo was most desirable. Many times when he had dropped in here for rest and food on his way down the trail, he had desired her. He might even marry her, the little kid. His eyes gloated over her, moved from her curly head to her small neat ankles in their long, laced boots.

'Jo,' he said softly. 'Suppose I say I want you to come along o' me — for good!'

She turned from the stove on which

she had set a pot of coffee. Eyed him steadily.

'No thanks, Conrad Owen.'

'Don't you like me?'

'Not much.'

'Damn it,' he said with a look of annoyance. 'The cheek of it.'

'Go out of this room and leave me to my cooking, please,' she said.

She was not prepared for his next move. He sprang at her suddenly, had her in his arms before she could prevent it. A feeling of acute terror gripped her then, she who was as a rule fearless. She felt his hot breath on her cold cheek and gasped.

'Let me go, Conrad Owen.'

'I want you,' he said. 'Look here, kid, I tell you straight, I'm mad for you. You're going to come along o' me — for good.'

'Never,' she said. 'Let me go. Beast . . . beast — let me go!'

He laughed and kissed her on the throat. She saw red then. Terror grew on her . . . terror of sex, of men . . . of her loneliness — the helplessness of a girl.

'Don't you dare to touch me,' she said. 'With my father lying dead in the next room. God should strike you dead . . . you beast!'

Her low furious voice sobered the man for an instant. He let her loose.

'Aw, cut it out, kid,' he said. 'I only want to be nice to you. A kiss or two. Come on now, my Beauty, be loving . . . '

Joanna gave him a look of scorn, pushed him from her and rushed out of the room. She heard him call her.

'Jo, come back, little fool. You can't escape me . . . '

Couldn't escape him? Couldn't she? Did he think she would stay here, now that she knew what he was like, what he wanted? He wanted her. She knew that he would not long have respect for the name of God or for a dead man. For the first time in her life she knew limitless terror. To be touched by that brute . . . she shuddered at the thought of his hot lips against her throat, knew she would die before she felt them on her lips. She must run . . . run for life itself.

It meant leaving Daddy . . . but Daddy would understand . . . she must get away from Conrad Owen. She dared not stay in this cabin with him tonight.

She fled through the living room and out of the cabin. She slammed the door behind her. She faced a stormy night. Icy flakes blinded her, beat against her face. But she did not notice the snow. She only heard the rough voice of the furtrader calling her.

'Come back you little . . . '

He called her a vile name which she barely understood.

She ran on . . . stumbling, panting . . . into the night.

2

For half-an-hour Joanna Grey made her way through the storm. Half mad with fear, but less afraid in the wilderness, in the storm, than she had been in the cabin with Conrad Owen and his clutching hands.

Dark spruce forest frowned on her. A frozen waterway. A starless sky, like a leaden pall and snow falling heavily. Desolation and darkness. And the girl, running, gasping, with a sharp pain in her side and nameless fear in her mind, seeking a safe hiding place from the man who was beast.

At last she slowed down, stopped, fell on to the snow in a little heap. Long shuddering sobs shook her.

'Oh! oh! oh! . . . ' she sobbed again and again.

She was exhausted, but she was still defiant. Even here, if she were lost and doomed to death in the wilderness, she had escaped from Conrad Owen and she did not think he would find her now.

Her shudders ceased. The small thin body in the fur coat twitched slightly and was still. The dark veil of insensibility had fallen over Joanna Grey. She was spent, done.

Along the frozen waterway toiled a team of dogs pulling a sled. A man wrapped in furs was driving them. Eyelashes, cheeks, lips, coated with crystals from his frozen breath.

He strained through the falling snow and saw the huddled body on the ground. He pulled up the team and sprang out.

'Hullo, what's this?' he muttered.

He pulled an electric torch from his pocket and flashed it on. Saw the thin body in the fur coat and leggings, the cropped curly head.

'A boy,' he said. 'A boy . . . half dead, I should think!'

Joanna stirred. She flung up her arm

and moaned, opened her eyes. Saw dimly the face of a man framed in a fur hood. For a moment thought it was Conrad Owen. She gave a cry.

'Don't touch me . . . '

Then she knew it was not Conrad Owen. He had a well-bred, unmistakably English voice. Like her father's had been. It said:

'All right, my lad. Don't be afraid. What's hurt you?'

She sat up, her heart pounding, and stared up through the whirling grey flakes at the stranger. 'My lad,' he said. Did he then think she was a boy? All the better if he did. She swallowed hard and stumbled on to her feet.

'I — want to get to — Fort Yukon,' she said.

'You're miles from there,' said the stranger. 'I'm going in the other direction. But you can come along with me if you like.'

She hesitated, stood wiping her smarting eyes with the back of her hand. She felt sick and dizzy. She said:

'Maybe you don't know this country. I do. We can't ride anywhere very far. A blizzard's coming up.'

A long wailing cry broke the stillness of the evening. A sad, hungry cry. It sent a shiver through Joanna.

'Wolf,' she said briefly.

'That being so,' said the man, 'we'd better move on. But what about you? How did you get out here like this?'

'Never mind,' she said. 'Let's find shelter.'

The man returned to his sled.

'Right,' he said.

She wanted to go back to the hut where she had left her father's body and dared not because of Conrad Owen. Kiche would return. Kiche must keep vigil for her. She must find shelter now with this stranger or die in the storm.

The dogs strained forward, leaping, snarling. They did not go far. They came to a small shanty built of spruce on the edge of the waterway. Joanna urged the man to stop.

'We can't go on in this blizzard,' she said.

'Very well, but I have little food,' he said.

She said nothing. He opened the door of the hut and struck a match, found an oil lamp and lit it. Joanna stumbled in and looked around her, brushing the snow from her eyes. The room was bare save for a wooden table, two chairs and a mattress with two torn blankets on the ground, and a small cooking-stove.

'I wonder who lived here,' she said. 'Perhaps someone dead or — gone on the trail.'

The man shut the door.

'It will keep out the cold if we light a fire and have some food, anyhow,' he said.

She watched him from under long lashes. He took off his fur cap and coat. She could see him plainly now for the first time. He was young, perhaps thirty. A spare athletic figure. Fine-cut face, a strong mouth and chin, brown hair. Handsome, in a stern fashion. And a man of intelligence and breeding. Unlike any other man she had seen out here. Dimly she recognised that quality of culture and appreciated it. It was not the face of a man who has gone lightly through life. She read repression in the stern lips and cynicism in the grey eyes. He had suffered.

He looked at her casually.

'Take off your furs, my lad. We've got to spend the night here, anyhow.'

'Yes,' she said, a slight tremor passing through her.

He pointed at the mattress.

'We can share that. Keep warm together under my fur rug off the sled.'

She pressed her hands tightly together but did not answer. She knew that sooner or later she must tell him that he was making a mistake and that she was not a boy. She remembered Conrad Owen's hot, grasping fingers and desirous eyes and she felt suddenly stiff with fear. If all men were alike. If this man . . . her

17

thoughts went no further. But she stood there in a frozen way, wondering if she had been a fool to come here and trust this stranger.

To hide her confusion she knelt down by the stove and began to rake the cinders with her bare hands. The man said:

'I'll get some wood for you . . . '

When he came back with a bundle of sodden twigs she was still kneeling there staring at the stove. Her head was spinning. She felt sick and dizzy, as though she were going to faint. She heard the man say:

'We'll have to put a dollop of kerosine on this wood to get it to light. What's wrong with you? Feeling sick?'

She tried to answer, then toppled over and lay on her side, gasping for breath.

'I — do feel rotten — faint — no food lately . . . don't touch me . . . ' she stammered incoherently.

The man dropped the wood and knelt beside her. He put an arm firmly beneath her and lifted her up.

'Come on, my boy, this won't do
— let's have a look at you — ' he began.

'Leave me alone,' Joanna said under
her breath, struggling desperately not to
faint.

Her words, her whole manner filled
the man with amazement. And he was
amazed by the light fragile weight of the
body in the curve of his arms. Suddenly
he pushed open her coat and his hand
touched her throat and breast. He felt
her trembling, heard her faint little
voice say: 'Don't . . . please don't . . . '

Then he knew that his companion
was a girl. It was a slender girl,
half-conscious, here in the hut with
him. For a moment in astonishment
and dismay he stared down at her. And
now as he saw the feminine curve of her
neck and the length of her lashes, he
wondered how he could have been such
a fool as to mistake her for a boy. Of
course the cropped curls and the
breeches had deceived him and who
would expect to find a girl out here?

The last thing he had wanted here in the wilderness was a woman . . . he had come to escape from a woman . . . to forget sex. Almost angrily he looked down at this girl, then whipped a flask out of his hip pocket and unscrewed the stopper. He forced the few drops of brandy between her lips. She choked and swallowed. The colour came back to her face, the red to her lips. She opened her eyes and began to move back from his supporting arm.

'Please let me go.'

'Look here, what are you frightened of?' he said. 'I know now you're a girl, but I'm not going to hurt you.'

She staggered on to her feet, stood looking up at him with wide bright eyes. His gaze travelled up and down the slim boyish figure. There was an angry flush on his face. He turned from her abruptly.

'I don't know what you think I am,' he added. 'But you're safe with me. You can have the mattress. I'll curl up on the floor. Now shall we light the fire?'

She drew a breath of relief; the hard throbbing of her heart died down. She felt that the dangerous moment had passed. She did not think she had anything to fear from this particular man. The brandy had given her fresh strength and she knelt down by the stove again and began to lay the fire.

Later when the fire was lit and the little cabin had grown hot and full of the odour of boiling coffee, the man and the girl sat down at the table and ate hungrily.

Over the meal they learned something about each other. Joanna told him of her father's death and the reason of her flight from the cabin. And he told her that his name was Richard Strange and that he had not come out to the Yukon for the reason most men come . . . for gold . . . but for forgetfulness. There were many things he wished to forget. But of these he did not speak, just then, to Joanna Grey. They were bitter and unhappy and he was a man of reticence.

He quite obviously disliked women and mistrusted them. Yet he looked with a certain pity at this young girl whom Fate had flung across his path. She was so very young, almost a child. She had led a rough, difficult life out here in the Yukon. She was a little savage, half educated, ignorant of the civilised world and its ways. While most girls of her age were still at school in the nursery, she had been keeping house in a rude log cabin on the frozen trail for her father. It was astonishing to Richard Strange that she should be as cultured as she was. John Grey had undoubtedly been a gentleman. There was that unmistakable quality of breeding in this child of the White Wilderness. Richard recognised that at once.

'It's incredible to me that any man could have kept you out here all these years . . . I mean, it's been a frightful life for a girl . . . ' he said, after he had listened to her story.

Joanna, who had taken off her fur coat and sat huddled before the stove, hands in the pockets of her old woolly jumper, looked at Richard Strange unsmilingly.

'Daddy couldn't help keeping me out here. He couldn't go back to England . . . he couldn't get work in any town like 'Frisco or New York. You see, poor darling Daddy had a weakness for drink and he had to keep away from the cities and temptations. And he always thought he'd strike gold up here one day.'

Richard liked the simplicity of that. This child had known her father's weakness and accepted it stoically. She was a grave stoic little creature.

'I see,' he said. 'And so he kept you with him. But it is no life for a girl out here.'

'Daddy brought me up as a boy.'

'I can tell that. All the same you are a girl.'

Joanna moved uneasily.

'I know, and when men like Conrad Owen . . . '

'Ah, there you are. There must be

many fellows of Conrad Owen's breed up in the Yukon . . . and anywhere else if it comes to that. You aren't safe. You oughtn't to be here.'

'I can take care of myself,' she said stubbornly.

Richard Strange took his pipe from his mouth and gave her a brief, frowning look.

'Up to a point. No further. What would have happened to you tonight if I hadn't found you?'

Joanna flushed.

She had no argument to that. But she liked to think she could take care of herself. It annoyed her to be treated by this stranger as though she were a silly baby.

'The best thing you can do is to get South as soon as you can,' he said, after a pause.

'I've no money and no one to go to,' said Joanna.

He stared.

'Then what on earth did you intend to do?'

'I know people in Fort Yukon and Dawson City. Friends of Daddy's. I might get a job.'

'What kind?'

'In one of the saloons, I suppose.'

Richard Strange leaned down and knocked the ash from his pipe.

'A child like you serving drinks in a saloon in the Yukon, eh?'

'I'm nineteen next spring.'

'Well, it doesn't seem right to me,' said Richard Strange. Then he lapsed into silence again, and scowled into the fire. After all, it was none of his business what this Joanna Grey did. And he wasn't going to make himself responsible for her welfare. She was a total stranger to him and she had lived most of her life out here. He presumed she knew a bit about it. On the other hand she was English and of gentle birth and it worried him a little. He didn't want to be worried over a nineteen year old girl . . . an orphan thrown on the world without a decent friend, without a farthing.

She had no relations that she knew of. A pity she wasn't a boy.

Joanna rose to her feet and he looked up at her. She was yawning, stretching her arms above her head like a healthy young animal ready for sleep. And now he saw, suddenly, beauty in the curve of her breasts under the tight-fitting woollen jumper, and the whole feminine grace of her. No boy, this. No child, either. She was a woman.

Once Richard Strange had loved women. As a very young man he had worshipped at the shrine of beauty. And to women he had been a charming lover, full of sensibility. Until one woman had ruthlessly destroyed every ideal and every belief. Today, at twenty-nine, he was a cynic, a man who could still be stirred, violently, by passion, but who had no longer any use for, or faith in, the thing called love.

Coming out here to the Yukon on the lonely, frozen trail, he had wanted to get away from all women. He was angry that he should find himself shut up in a hut with this girl, Joanna.

'How long might this blizzard last?' he asked her.

'Oh, a long time — many days.'

'Damn,' he said under his breath.

Joanna heard him. She coloured.

'It's just as aggravating for me,' she said.

'Quite,' he said with a grim smile.

He turned his gaze from her and packed another pipe. And while he smoked he was conscious of her presence and strangely embarrassed by it.

'One thinks one can put women out of one's life,' he pondered. 'But it's impossible.'

Joanna was puzzled by his demeanour.

'He's a queer rude man,' she thought.

She had never met another man like Richard Strange. He treated her as though he almost disliked her. Still, that was preferable to the company of Conrad Owen and his kind.

She grew very tired and kept yawning and shutting her eyes. She must share this room with this man tonight, whatever he was. There was only one bed. What would he do?

Her heart gave a jerk when at last Richard Strange put his pipe in his pocket, stretched and rose.

'It's about time we turned in,' he said.

'Yes,' she said.

She stood before him, her hands locked behind her. He glanced at her and saw that she was nervous and that her cheeks were hot and red. She was very woman then, disturbing his peace.

'Oh, damn it all,' he thought angrily. 'Does she think all men are like this Owen?'

'You take the mattress and the blankets,' he said curtly.

'Thank you,' she said. The galloping of her heart died down a little. She added, like a grateful child. 'Thanks awfully.'

'What did you think would happen?' he said in a rough voice.

Joanna went scarlet.

'I — nothing — oh, I — ' she broke off and bit at her lip as though she were going to cry.

And Richard Strange, who could never bear to see a woman cry, hated himself for being so rude and unchivalrous. The child had been badly treated by the fellow back in her father's cabin . . . badly scared. No wonder she was scared now, and suspicious. He felt a sudden wish to be gentle with her.

'You tuck up and go to sleep, old thing,' he said. 'And don't be afraid of me. I'm going to take the robes from the sled over the other side of the room. Goodnight.'

He gave her a half-smile and Joanna was amazed to see how that smile softened his hard face and how attractive his eyes were when he looked like that. She wanted somebody to be like that tonight, just friendly and kind. A lump came into her throat but she did not cry. She said:

'Goodnight.' Then turned and lay down on the mattress and covered herself with the blankets.

Strange blew out the lamp and settled himself on some furs on the other side of the room which was dark now except for a dull red glow from the dying fire.

Joanna looked at him, peered over the rim of the blankets and thought how uncomfortable he must be. It was kind of him to give her the mattress. What a curious man he was. How awfully nice he could be . . . when he wanted. She tried to sleep and found it hard for a while. The woman in her, so terrified of Conrad Owen, was still a little frightened of this Englishman. She kept opening her tired eyes to look at him, to wonder if he slept. Once when he stirred, her heart leapt furiously. But he said nothing and she could not see his face in the darkness. She could only hear his breathing.

At last she slept.

It was the man who lay longest awake. He was thinking of women and knowing how impossible it was for him to forget that the attraction between the sexes is the most vital and insistent thing in the world. When he heard

Joanna's soft, regular breathing and knew she was asleep, he smiled grimly to himself.

'Richard, you poor fool, that girl isn't half so afraid of you as you are of her. Damn it, let's hope the blizzard ends tomorrow.'

3

But the blizzard raged on and for five days and five nights the man and the girl were shut up in the cabin unable to move out.

Richard Strange fretted and fumed. He wanted to go on — carry out his scheme of things. In that scheme women played no part. And here he was shut up in one single room with a girl who unconsciously made a direct appeal to him.

Physically Joanna was very attractive. She was fresh and unspoiled and charming with her healthy, graceful young body and dark, beautiful eyes and cropped curly head. But it was her character that he most admired. He could not remain shut up with her for days and nights without discovering her many admirable traits. She had pluck and spirit and reserve and a certain fierce, virginal purity and pride which he must, necessarily, appreciate. She had learned a hard lesson up here in the North and it seemed to him that her life, so empty of fun and laughter and the normal pleasures of a young girl, had been nothing less than a tragedy.

But never once did he hear her whine or complain. She accepted hardships as they came. She had none of the exigence, the irritating whims of the woman who had ruined Richard Strange's life. She made no demands. She took the small portions of food which he was forced to share out very sparingly, day by day, and ate without complaining. She swept and dusted the little cabin every morning as best she could with a dilapidated old broom and a plate for a dustpan. She was as scrupulously clean as she could be under the difficult circumstances. Her first thought when she awoke was to put some snow water on the little stove and wash herself, keep her hair combed, her nails clean.

'Some women might let themselves go out here in this frightful place . . . but Joanna doesn't,' Richard thought.

He found her as gallant as any boy and could not fail to soften toward her because of it. He admired a brave spirit before anything else in the world. He was no longer rude to her or brusque in his manner. After their first twenty-four hours of enforced companionship he treated her as he might have treated a man, a young partner on the trail. He talked to her, laughed with her, helped her to wash up their bits of crockery and once or twice was awake before she roused and ready with a cup of hot coffee when she opened her eyes.

Joanna began to like this man very much indeed. Her fear of him vanished utterly. She learned to talk to him. She had never really had anybody to talk to except Daddy who had loved her but been too old and embittered by life to give her companionship such as Richard Strange could give. He, under a thin layer of cynicism, was eager for adventure and anxious that life should be a jest instead of a stern drama.

They laughed, they joked together, these two who had been thrown together so unexpectedly. It was inevitable they should lose a certain amount of reserve and grow intimate and friendly with each other.

Joanna found, too, that she could learn much from Richard. He had much to tell. All that he had to say interested her vastly. But his stories were always impersonal. He continued to be reticent about his private affairs. She only knew that he had been educated at Rugby and that was a bond, because Daddy had been a Rugby man. And he had been to Oxford and he got his rowing Blue and he had been out East and made a lot of money growing coffee and tea. He had come back from Ceylon a year ago comparatively a rich man. When Joanna asked curiously why he bothered to hit this hard frozen trail if he was not in need of money, he shut up like a clam and gave her a brief, non-committal reply.

Night after night while the blizzard raged furiously round the little cabin, when their supper was finished, Richard smoked his pipe before the stove and Joanna sat at his feet, curled up like a child, listening to his stories of England and all the things she had heard of, read of, but never done. Never until now had she realised how isolated, how empty her existence was out here in the Yukon.

Richard became accustomed to these evenings . . . even grew to like them. There was a certain fascination in educating Joanna . . . watching the wonder grow in her great brown eyes which were fixed so raptly, so intently upon him.

He treated her like his little comrade . . . but beneath the pluck, the endurance of her lay the woman . . . and in her soft moods — the moods which made her curl up at his feet and lean her elbow on his knees and talk to him

— he found her very disturbing to his peace.

'Whatever I do I mustn't make love to her,' he thought as the hours and days and nights passed and still they remained snowed up . . . growing more intimate, more interested each in the other.

But he found it difficult to control the sudden violent longing that possessed him to draw the slim little figure up into his arms and show her that men and women can create heaven on earth, and, occasionally, climb to the stars.

He knew her so well now. She was essentially innocent although she knew all the facts of life and could defend herself. Underneath she was, also, essentially passionate and Richard Strange who knew and understood women . . . realised this fact . . . and was certain that when Joanna Grey loved it would be with tremendous courage and sincerity. Above all things, she would be loyal.

When these difficult, fierce moods swept the man, the solitude and imprisonment with the girl became torment to him. And torment made him curt with her again. She, scarcely comprehending, was hurt. Twice he drew away from her when she sat at his feet and leaned against his knees. Twice when she held out a hand with almost a boy's gesture of affection, to say 'Goodnight, Richard' . . . he did not take it. Only said 'Goodnight, Jo . . . ' and seemed to her morose and bored.

He had become to her the most wonderful man in the world and she could not bear the idea that he was bored with her and sick to death of the unending storm, the storm no longer mattered to her. Neither had she any more that frantic longing to get back to her old home and to Kiche. She wanted to sit at the feet of Richard Strange — forever.

When he saw the hurt look on her face, he had to trample on his desire to take her in his arms and comfort her. For hours he would lie awake, staring angrily through the darkness, ruminating on the freakish tricks Fate plays

38

upon human beings.

Food was getting scarce. The whole situation was becoming fraught with a new danger now. The blizzard raged on and the store of Richard's tinned stuff was gradually diminishing. The oil gave out altogether. Then they had to sit in total darkness after sunset and shiver without a fire.

Joanna bore this cruel discomfort with a fortitude before which the man bowed.

'You're game, little Anna,' he said to her one night in a burst of admiration which he could not repress. 'Damn it, few women would put up with this show and not whine.'

'But I'm quite happy,' she said. Then added, with an almost wistful look at him: 'Anna is a new name for me, isn't it?'

'I've decided to call you Anna,' he said. 'I like it. Joanna is too stately — Jo is too masculine — to me you're just little Anna.'

She laughed.

'No one's ever called me that before,'

she said. 'I like it.'

'And what shall we do if food runs out, little Anna?' he said.

'It will last. Why I had a huge helping of corned beef for dinner,' she said.

She was gallant. He knew her portion had been small. But his own had been very much smaller. Unknown to her he was giving her more than half his own share every day. He was very hungry but he preferred to go short rather than that this brave child should endure the tortures of hunger.

'Well, I daresay we shall come out alive,' he said. 'The storm can't last forever.'

'And when we can get away, we'll just say goodbye and you'll carry on your trail?' said Joanna.

'Yes,' he said.

The pain that rent Joanna's heart then was very much sharper and crueller than the pang of physical hunger could have been. But Richard didn't know it.

They could neither of them see each other. It was so bitterly cold, they had lain down and covered themselves with rugs long before bedtime.

Then, suddenly, a little groan was wrung from her.

Richard sat up, his eyes straining to see her.

'Anna, what is it, child?'

'Nothing,' she said with a half-shamed laugh. 'Only my hands and feet are so frightfully cold, I can't sleep.'

Before he could stop himself he had crossed to her mattress and felt for her hands. He grasped them, exclaiming as he felt how icy-cold they were, blew on them, rubbed them, tried to make them warm. He could not see her but he could feel her breath on his cheek. She said in a shy little voice:

'Thanks, awfully, Richard. Good-night.'

The most terrible temptation seized Richard Strange . . . to pull her into his arms, bury his face against the warm whiteness of her young throat, kiss

her until she burned with his kisses.
Joanna suddenly sensed that something was wrong with him . . . he
crouched there by her so silently. Her
hands hurt from the fierce pressure of
his hands. And her own heart began
to pound. Something vividly alive
. . . almost electric . . . darted between
them in this moment. They were
acutely conscious of each other. To
Joanna, it was a strange emotion that
gripped her. She hardly understood
the chaos of it, but it seemed to her
very apparent that she loved this man
. . . not as she had loved Daddy or
any man she had ever known . . . that
she was half-afraid of him, yet would
die of rapture if he made love to her,
tonight.

He broke the tense silence.

'I hate you to feel cold, Anna . . . '

'I'm all right now,' she stammered.
'Go back to bed.'

He suddenly crushed the little hands
against his lips. She began to tremble.

'Go back — to bed,' she repeated in

vague ecstasy and terror.

Somehow he managed to drag himself away and return to his own side of the cabin. But he was shaking and he lay there, sleepless, praying fiercely for daylight. He knew this state of affairs could not go on.

Two nights later he fainted from lack of food and she, suddenly seeing the pallor of his cheeks, the hollows, realised that he was starving. She dragged the truth out of him, knew that he had been denying himself food in order to make it last longer for her. She knew, too, that all food had come to an end and that unless the blizzard ended, they would face death. They had been here ten days and ten nights.

Richard recovered from his fainting fit. He sat in a chair before the unlit stove. It was bitterly cold. Joanna herself felt half-frozen and hungry. But she forgot that. She could only stare up at Richard's haggard face and remember what sacrifices this man had made for her.

'Oh, Richard!' she said. 'Richard . . . why did you do it . . . why have you starved yourself for me?'

'I'm all right, little Anna,' he said.

But she, who never cried, was crying now — tears poured down her cheeks. And then the man seemed to break with her. He pulled her up into his arms with fierce sad passion.

'Oh, darling little thing, don't cry!'

She clung to him shuddering with sobs. She knew that she loved him. This was the one thing, the only thing in life, this consuming passion for him . . . a passion that lifted her out of herself, knew no pride, only the absorbing wish to give and give to her lover.

'Richard . . . Richard,' she said.

His lips were against her mouth, his hand caressing her hair.

'I've wanted you madly . . . days and nights . . . oh, terrible hours, Joanna . . . loved you, wanted you. Do you understand now? That night when you were cold, I wanted to take you in my arms like this. I tried not to. I have no right to now. But I love you so . . . kiss me . . . kiss me, my dear!'

Love drenched and drowned them . . . they clung to each other. Very close he held her with a strength born of his love. Kissed the tears from her lashes, then drank in the sweetness of her mouth with a long kiss that shivered through her body like a flame.

Her eyelids closed, her arms curved about his neck. Her fierce spirit was tamed while she lay in his arms.

At last he raised his head; he pressed his cheek to her short curls.

'Dearest,' he said. 'How I love you.'

'I love you,' she said. 'I love you.'

He held her closer.

'Little Anna, this is a terrible, wonderful thing. You have brought back all the beauty and splendour of living to me. I thought I should never care for a woman again. But you . . . my little love . . . so brave, so dear . . . I can't help loving you.'

'Does it matter?' she whispered.

He gave a broken laugh. Looked down at her rapt young face ... the vision of her growing strangely dim with every passing moment as his feeble strength ebbed from him. He said:

'My dear, my sweet, I've got to tell you now. I'm married.'

'Married,' she repeated. She shivered a little, then pressed her lips to his shoulder. 'Oh, Richard, are you?'

'Yes. Don't blame me, darling, if I have been weak. I couldn't help telling you I loved you.'

She shut her eyes.

'Richard, nothing matters. You have taught me how to live, how to be happy, and I love you.'

'But what can I do, little Anna?'

'If we live,' she said. 'If we get out of this alive, I suppose you will have to leave me again. But at least I shall have had your love for a bit.'

'Oh, my darling, my dear ... '

They kissed again — she clung close, her hands about his head, her heart beating frantically.

'I must tell you about my wife,' he said in a slow painful voice. 'It's only right you should hear and judge . . . for yourself.'

'Yes, tell me,' she said.

She leaned her head against his shoulder and he held her closer. He told her the history of his marriage.

4

'Such an old, hackneyed tale, little Anna,' he said. 'A complete failure . . . and God knows I've seen many others around me. You see . . . I was a boy of twenty-three, out in Ceylon. I can look back now and see what an impulsive, idealistic fool I was . . . ' He gave a bitter laugh, his hand caressed Joanna's head. She lay very still and mute against him, listening. 'I idealised all women and after the death of my mother, whom I had adored, I wanted a woman in my life. I was lonely — on my plantation in Ceylon there wasn't a soul to speak to except Digby, my partner, who was a much older man than myself and not particularly cheerful. I was bored when I wasn't working. And that climate and the loneliness plays the dickens with a man's nerves. Then Digby sent for his daughter,

Madge. She came out for a month's holiday. She was very good-looking in a rather cold way . . . rather like a statue . . . very pale . . . aquiline features . . . blue eyes and blonde hair, rather wonderful hair which she hadn't bobbed like most women. It hung below her waist when it was down.'

Richard paused. A little tremor went through the girl in his arms.

'And this — Madge — became — your wife?' she whispered.

'Yes, Anna. She was very nice to me. She set herself out to be charming. She was three years older than I was but that didn't make any difference. She saw how damned lonely and fed-up I was and she seemed to want to get married. I fell in love with her. It was my first serious affair and I thought Madge was wonderful and she seemed to make life quite a different thing out there in Ceylon. Digby made no objection and there it was . . . I rushed into marriage.'

'I see,' whispered Joanna.

And because she had a vivid imagination, she thought she could visualise the whole thing. Richard, the young, enthusiastic Richard, the idealist, even the romantic, swept away on a tide of passion for his partner's daughter. It hadn't been real love. Just loneliness, passion, and the response of an inexperienced boy to a woman older than himself, who was nice to him.

Richard continued his story.

That marriage had been doomed from the outset. Within a few days of their wedding out East, Madge had shown what she really was. A cold superior young woman, censorious of the impulsive boy she had married, devoid of passion, herself, but exacting homage and admiration, exigent to the last degree.

At first Richard had lavished all his hot-headed devotion upon her. He had been proud of her. No man could help admiring her blonde, patrician looks and her tall, fine figure. And she had gifts. She played the piano well, sang a little, made an excellent hostess. The men in Ceylon liked and admired her.

But for Richard and all men Madge had only her cold, superior smile and she accepted her husband's passionate devotion, at first in a patronising fashion, then with passive indifference. At the end of the first six months she was telling him that she hated love-making and made it plain that his kisses, his caresses bored, even repelled her.

Her attitude had the natural effect of killing Richard's passion completely and absolutely. He swung round from that charming impulsive love which he had first given her to something approaching dislike. Finally, she made it so plain that she had only married him because she had been bored as Miss Digby; had wanted a home of her own; that Richard lost all his desire to win any response from her. They grew antagonistic and began to quarrel. When old Digby died and Richard and Madge were alone on the estate, things went from bad to worse. Richard became sullen, morose. He admitted it. Madge criticised him and nagged at him. Half crazy with irritation and disappointment, he asked for his release. She refused to give it to him. She was the dog in the manger. She didn't want to lead the normal passionate life of a happily-married woman, but she was proud of Richard's good looks and his popularity in the East and his position which was rapidly improving. She did not intend to give him up.

'She has one of those queer, perverse, jealous temperaments,' Richard told Joanna. 'Couldn't bear me to look at another woman, mark you, yet didn't really want me herself. Well, I'd married her and I was still something of an idealist and I didn't believe in divorce. I don't think I do now. It's wrong to wriggle out of one's contracts, however much one regrets signing them. But the thing I most regretted was having no child. I wanted a kid badly.'

Joanna suddenly hugged him. Tears stung her eyelids.

'Oh, Richard, poor darling Richard.'

'Well, Madge was terrified of having a baby and that ended that dream,' he said with a terse laugh. 'We continued to exist together . . . for six years. A feat of endurance on my part, I assure you. I ached for freedom. But Madge kept me chained to her and I continued to think it my duty to stay while she wanted me. I worked like the dickens — work kept me from suicide, I think — and I made a lot of money and we left Ceylon and came home . . . bought a house in Chelsea. Things seemed a bit better. Madge interested herself in her music. She had a sort of studio and a lot of friends. But I tell you, little Anna, she was the coldest creature I think I've ever met . . . ice-cold. There wasn't any warmth, any intimacy in our companionship. Sometimes I found it damned difficult to be civil to her when she was in her sarcastic moods, telling me how uncontrolled I was.'

'You,' said Joanna in an indignant voice. '*You*, uncontrolled . . . when I think of these last ten days . . . '

She broke off and seized one of his hands and laid her warm lips against the wrist.

'Oh, my dear,' he said. 'I admit it hasn't been easy. You're like a little flame . . . so beautifully human and natural and wonderful. You are all that I have ever wanted or dreamed about. If I'd met you, six years ago . . . '

He broke off, sighing wearily. He pressed his cheek to hers. He wished he did not feel so weak, so faint. It was lack of food, of course. The room seemed to go round and round, occasionally. He tightened his clasp of Joanna and shut his eyes. He told her the rest of the story.

How, finally, three months ago, he had rebelled fiercely against the life he was leading in London and had decided to travel. Madge insisted on coming with him. They travelled to America through California. Then Richard had conceived an immense longing for solitude, for hitting a lonely trail, up North where the cold and hardships would be in a measure an anodyne for the torment of irritation he had been forced to endure in the company of his wife.

When he told Madge he was going to leave her she was very annoyed, but for once he was adamant and he left her, piqued and furious, in 'Frisco.

'I told her I was sailing to Nome and then going up the river to the Yukon trail and I left her in a luxurious hotel with plenty to amuse her,' finished Richard grimly. 'But I simply had to get away, my dear. I had to.'

'I understand,' said Joanna. 'I think I would feel like that, tied up to someone who wasn't in sympathy with me.'

'But I assure you, her nature is so warped, so unreasonably jealous, it's as likely as not she'd follow me — hit the trail herself, just to show me I couldn't escape her,' he said in a sardonic voice.

'Oh, Richard . . . if she turns up . . . '

'Don't even think about it. I couldn't bear it. Anna, everything has changed . . . all my feelings about life . . . now I've met you. I love you so tremendously, you little, brave, vital thing . . .'

'Richard, I adore you.'

'Confound my head,' he muttered. 'It's spinning again, Anna, I mustn't be ill . . . don't let me be ill.'

'You've had nothing to eat. Oh, Richard,' she touched his face, his forehead. 'You're frozen and weak because you've given me all your food. Oh, *Richard* . . .'

'Don't worry . . . little Anna . . .'

He broke off. His arms fell away from her. He swayed and toppled from his chair. She only just had time to detach herself from his arms, otherwise he would have pulled her down with him. She went down on her knees beside him.

'Richard . . . darling, darling Richard . . .'

But his eyes were closed and his lips murmured unintelligible things. He was starving, half-conscious. His flash of strength had gone.

She chafed his hands between her own, kissed them wildly.

'Richard, darling, darling Richard, don't leave me now. Oh, what can I do?'

She sprang up, looked desperately about her. No food, no coffee, nothing left. And Richard would die of hunger. If so, she prayed that she would follow quickly. There was nothing, nobody in life for her now, but Richard. Just for the moment his wife did not exist in her mind. He loved her, and they were together . . . and perhaps this was the end of all things for them both.

And then, suddenly, she heard the sound of men's voices and the snarling of dogs. Hope gripped her once more. Perhaps the blizzard was over, had ceased this last hour. She could get help for Richard and for herself. Somebody was coming, anyhow . . . traders, maybe, to give her food for Richard.

She opened the door.

A cry escaped her and she shrank back. A man, carrying a lantern stood there, a man in a bearskin coat. It was Conrad Owen. Another man was with him, a small, thin man whom she did not know.

She stood staring. Conrad Owen flashed the light on her. He gave a cry.

'Great guns, it's Joanna Grey herself.'

'What . . . Joanna Grey?' said the man who followed Conrad into the hut. 'But how strange, what a coincidence!'

'So this is where you've been hiding, eh?' said Conrad. He set the lantern on the table and stared round. He saw Richard Strange's figure on the floor. 'Why, say, what's this?'

'He's starving,' said Joanna. 'We've been shut up here in the blizzard. Conrad, you've got food outside . . . brandy or whisky . . . something . . . give it to him quickly.'

Conrad gave her a quick searching look. Then he threw the light on the face of the man who was muttering, weakly, in delirium. He gave a long whistle.

'Damme if it isn't that fine Englishman that I met in the bar up at Fort

Yukon a few weeks back.'

'You know him?' said Joanna.

'Know him!' Conrad gave an ugly laugh. 'He caught me a swipe over the mouth because I tried to kiss Sal Pilcher. I said I'd pay him out for it and so I will.'

He kicked the prostrate man suddenly, brutally. Richard stirred and groaned. Like a wildcat Joanna flew at Conrad, struck him with clenched fists.

'Beast, beast . . . to kick him. Oh, you great bully. Don't dare touch him.'

'Hello, hello,' said Conrad. 'Special pal of yours, eh, Jo?'

Panting, she swung round to the stranger.

'I don't know who you are, but I appeal to you to give me food for my . . . my friend.'

The man eyed her uneasily, coughed. Conrad laughed again.

'Let me introduce you, Jo. Mr. James Spence, my pal. James, this is little Jo, and she's going to marry me.'

'It's a lie,' said Joanna, her face white

as a sheet. 'A lie!'

Conrad moved across the cabin to the other man. Joanna went down on her knees beside Richard.

'Richard, Richard, wake up!' she sobbed.

But Richard Strange, who loved her and would have given anything on earth to protect her from these men, lay helpless. He was no longer conscious.

Conrad spoke in a low tone to the man whom he called James Spence.

'See here, now we've found the girl, we don't want to let this blasted Englishman interfere. I'm not going to leave him food. He can stay here and die.'

Spence fingered his moustache.

'It's something like murder, Owen.'

'Hell to that,' said Conrad. 'If he starves it's not my affair. We want this girl. We take her . . . right now. You agreed. It's our bargain.'

'Huh . . . that's so,' said Spence feebly.

Forty-eight hours ago Conrad Owen had found James Spence at Fort Yukon, looking for the Greys. He had been sent out from England to look for them. He told Conrad that old William Grey, Joanna's grandfather, had died, forgiving his black sheep son, and had left his money to John Grey. So Joanna was an heiress now, a rich young woman, and James Spence had been sent by old Grey's executor to find her.

Spence was a rogue. He had few scruples and he needed money. Conrad Owen wanted money, and he also wanted Joanna Grey. A despicable bargain was struck between them. If Conrad should help James Spence to find Joanna, James Spence would help Conrad to marry the girl and they should share her money.

Joanna, unconscious of the value set on her innocent head, knelt by Richard and implored him to speak to her. Conrad Owen came across the cabin and picked her up in his arms.

'You ain't going to stay howling by that guy. You're coming along to Fort

Yukon with me and Mr. Spence,' he said.

She kicked him . . . eyes blazing . . . wild with fear and hatred.

'Let me go. Don't — oh, don't . . . Richard . . . Richard . . . '

'Come on, Spence,' said Owen.

He carried Joanna in his great arms, out of the hut into the night. The snow was no longer falling. The spruce forest loomed before them, still and powdered white. The wind had dropped. A large sled with a big team of wolf-dogs waited for them.

When Joanna realised that she was being virtually kidnapped by these men and taken from Richard, she was like one demented. She bruised and hurt herself, struggling, screamed hoarsely, beat at Conrad Owen's face with her clenched knuckles. He only laughed at her.

'You lie still, Beauty. You're coming with me, now.'

'Let me go . . . you can't take me . . . you can't leave Mr. Strange . . . he'll die . . . he's starving. I tell you!' she sobbed wildly, incoherently.

'Let him die,' said Conrad.

Joanna thought of Richard, lying there, deserted; thought of him dying, alone, wretchedly. And she loved him, she had learnt passion and ecstasy in his arms. It was more than she could endure to know that she might never see him again on this earth.

The sled moved away swiftly over the frozen ground, leaving the little hut far behind.

5

It was Conrad's scheme to take Joanna Grey to Fort Yukon then to Nome and there get a steamer going Southland and finally land her in San Francisco before taking the final journey home.

Conrad meant to force little Jo into marriage with him before they left America to settle up her grandfather's estate.

But Conrad forgot that he had no weakly, hysterical girl to deal with and that Joanna Grey had been bred in the Klondike; that she was a young, strong, fearless creature full of fierce pride and courage. A woman to hold her own.

Only for the first few miles Joanna gave way to hysterical grief. Then she grew quiet. The tears dried on her lashes. She stared with frozen calm at the grim, stark snow-white country over which they were travelling, drawn by a fast pack of dogs. She knew what she meant to do. Nothing on earth would make her stay with Conrad Owen and this horrible friend of his. She did not care whether Richard was married or not. She was going back to him. Her place was with him. She had nobody else in the world.

Just why Conrad Owen and this man, James Spence, were so anxious to take her with them she did not trouble to wonder. She knew nothing of her grandfather's fortune nor of Conrad's schemes. Her feelings out in this primitive country were primitive. She hated Conrad; was afraid of him. She loved Richard and to Richard she would belong. Besides, at the moment she could only visualise him dying of hunger in that hut and she felt wild with fear . . .

It seemed to her that they travelled an interminable distance before they stopped. And the further they went, the lower her heart sank. Miles and miles of snow and frozen space between her and her lover now.

But her spirits rose again when they reached a settlement where there were cabins; much food and a general atmosphere of excitement. This was a meeting-place of fur-traders; of Indians and white men who were setting out for Dawson and the Klondike . . . gold-hunters from all parts of the world.

Joanna knew this settlement. She had been here with her father. She also knew that Kiche, her trusted Indian servant had come here to fetch the priest for the burial of her father. Maybe she would find Kiche here.

Conrad Owen lifted her out of the sled and carried her into a large drinking saloon which was also a rough and primitive hostel. Here men could get food and whisky and there were one or two women ready to dance; and beds for rest. The place was full to overflowing, tonight. The blizzard had stopped and men who had been unable to move for days — like Joanna and Richard — had come out at last.

Joanna went through a bad hour. She

was given food and drink for which she was grateful. She was half-starving. But she could think of nothing but Richard . . . Richard who had starved himself for her. She wanted him desperately. Desperately wanted to get back to that little cabin in the wilderness.

Conrad Owen kept a firm, possessive hand on her; introduced her to all the traders, the men he knew, as his 'girl'. Her protests were only met with loud guffaws of laughter. Out here nobody had time to meddle with other people's affairs and if Conrad said the girl belonged to him, then she did and if a fellow tried to interfere he might get a bullet in him. So who would argue about it?

She was given no chance of escape that night.

Conrad was friendly with a woman who was married to Bill Anstey, the man who owned the hostel. This woman, Mattie, had a dollar-bill slipped into her hand by Conrad and the hint that the slim little dark-eyed girl in her fur coat and breeches, was to be kept in sight.

Twice Joanna tried to creep out of the bedroom which she had to share with Mattie. Twice, Mattie pulled her back and said:

'Aw, kid, stay where you are. You're Conrad Owen's girl and you don't wanna go chasin' round nowhere else.'

Joanna found it useless to argue with the woman who was a coarse, unsympathetic creature brutalised by the life she had led up in the Yukon for the last twenty-five years. She had no sleep that night. She lay wide awake, staring with tearless eyes into the darkness, wondering whether Richard was alive or dead. She kept on repeating his name to herself:

'Richard . . . Richard . . . '

She felt she would go mad if she never saw him again; to think of him dying there, alone, unattended . . . it was frightful.

When the dawn came, and Mrs. Anstey was snoring on her camp bed at the other side of the dirty, untidy bedroom, Joanna rose; stretched her cramped limbs and walked to the window. She looked out. It was a brilliant morning, freezing hard; but sunshine flooded the white wilderness. The snow-covered ground scintillated like encrusted diamonds. Another week and spring would be here. The great thaw would flood the rivers and the break up of the ice would begin.

Suddenly Joanna's face flamed and hope surged through her. She saw the figure of an Indian standing by a team of dogs. His stoic, brown-red face in its frame of lank black hair was familiar to her. Kiche . . . Kiche . . . Daddy's Indian.

She looked at Mattie — every nerve in her body aquiver. The woman slept heavily. Then Joanna acted with all speed. She opened the square little windows noiselessly and called to the Indian.

'Kiche . . . Kiche!'

He started and turned to her. When

he saw her, he broke into a beaming smile and hurried to her. She put a finger to her lips.

'Ssh . . . quietly, Kiche. I've been brought here by Conrad Owen. But I want to get away. Kiche, you must take me . . . '

'Kiche always take little White Mistress anywhere,' the man said eagerly. 'Been waiting here, looking for you. Master buried many days ago.'

Joanna's eyes stung with hot tears. But there was no time now to ask Kiche for details of that burial or explain her absence. She hoisted herself up on to the sill; gave Kiche her hand; and the next moment he drew her safely through. She jumped down on to the crunching snow.

'Quickly, Kiche . . . the sled . . . we must get away. Have you food?'

'Yes, plenty food,' said the Indian.

'Then in the direction of home. There is a cabin we must find. I think I know where it is. Straight down the waterway, Kiche. There is a white man there, starving.'

She was bright-eyed, glowing, triumphant as the Indian whipped up his dogs and they leapt away from the hostel. She had outwitted Conrad Owen. When he awoke he would find her gone. And now, with Kiche to protect her, he should not get her again.

She was like one frenzied with eagerness and anxiety when she directed Kiche to the hut where she had been snowed up with Richard. They found it. Her heart leaped madly. She sprang out of the sled and rushed toward the little cabin; drawing off her mittens.

'Oh, God, I must be in time to save him . . . I must,' she thought. 'Richard . . . my dear . . . my dear!'

She flung open the cabin door. She stopped dead on the threshold, blinking as she came out of the bright sunlight. She saw a woman in the cabin . . . a woman stirring something in a bowl on the stove which was alight. Richard lay on the mattress. He was sleeping.

Joanna's heart seemed to stand still. She stared blankly at the woman. A tall fine figure; with a cold, clear-cut face and fair hair plaited above her head. She wore a leather coat with fur collar buttoned tightly above her throat.

Joanna's gaze, travelling amazedly round the room saw many things that had not been there yesterday. Boxes; stacks of tinned food; blankets, and a regular camping-outfit of canvas things.

Then she turned to the man on the mattress and everything else faded from her mind. She ran to him.

'Richard! Richard!' she said.

The woman put the bowl on the table.

'May I ask who you are?' she said.

But Joanna was oblivious of her; blind; deaf to everybody but Richard who had stirred and opened his eyes as she spoke his name.

'Richard,' she said again, 'I've come back.'

'Anna,' he said in a feeble voice. 'My dear . . . '

'Pardon me,' said the fair-haired woman behind Joanna, 'but I haven't the slightest idea who you are. I'm Mrs. Richard Strange. I managed to trace my husband here late last night. It seems to me just as well. He was half dying.'

Joanna turned her head and looked up at the other woman — dumbly. Then she said in an unbelieving voice:

'You are — Richard's wife?'

'Yes, do you mind?' said Madge Strange sarcastically.

'Do I mind?' repeated Joanna slowly. She knit her brows. She was used to straight talk; to the blunt, direct truth of the North. Not to sarcasm. She read nothing but hostility in Mrs. Strange's blue eyes. She flushed scarlet, and stared at Richard again, in a helpless way.

'Anna,' came the feeble voice from the mattress again. 'Anna.'

Joanna went to him at once. She placed both small, cold little hands in his. The tears poured down her cheeks. Always tears for him . . . tears that he alone had power to stir from the very fount of things. She said:

'Thank God you're all right . . . oh, Richard, I thought you were dead!'

'Very near it,' he said. She saw how ghastly ill he looked; hollow about the cheeks and eyes. He had starved himself for days . . . for her sake. She was torn with gratitude, with grief that he should have come to this — through her. She repeated:

'Thank God you're all right again.'

'My wife turned up in the nick of time . . . ' he gave a short, unhappy laugh. 'I told you I thought she'd follow me. Perhaps it would have been better for us all if she'd let me die.'

'No, no, no!' said Joanna. She shuddered, 'No, Richard — never!'

'How did you get back? I was only half-conscious when you went away. I realised, vaguely, that somebody had come and taken you . . . I heard you scream. It was frightful, Anna. I couldn't move or speak; hadn't even the power to open my eyes. I just knew you were going . . . against your will. As though it were thousands of miles away,

I heard you . . . and couldn't get to you. It was frightful,' he repeated.

She swallowed hard.

'It was Conrad Owen and another man. They kidnapped me. But I got away at Fort Yukon. Kiche helped me.'

'Pardon me,' came Madge Strange's cold, drawling voice. 'Might I interrupt this charming scene of reunion and have some explanation of who you are . . . how you come to be on such familiar terms with my husband?'

Joanna turned round to her. She faced Richard Strange's wife. Like a boy, she dashed the tears from her eyes with the back of one slim hand. She was no weakling unable to defend herself. She had known very few women in her life. The hard, austere existence up here in the frozen North which had placed her almost entirely in the company of men. But she found it difficult to deal with a woman like this one; an educated, cultured English-woman. On the other hand Joanna was first and foremost a creature of pride and spirit. She would allow nobody to talk to her in this sarcastic fashion. She flung back her head.

'I am Joanna Grey. Richard and I were snowed up here during the big blizzard. That's why I know him.'

Richard Strange raised himself weakly on one elbow. His thin face was drawn with the strain from which he had barely had time to recover. He looked at the two women. The one who was his wife. The one whom he had grown to love more than life itself. He said:

'Madge . . . I wanted to tell you . . . about little Anna. But I haven't had a chance. I've been so damned weak. Listen — '

'Please, Richard, lie down and compose yourself,' Madge broke in. She crossed to his side and pushed him back on to the pillow. He was yet so weak that he could not resist her. 'I'll deal with this young woman.'

'I don't think so,' said Joanna swiftly. Sudden rage possessed her. Her small body quivered. 'I'm not used to being *dealt with* by anybody. You are Richard's wife. I've no right to stay here now. I'll go . . . '

She swung round on her heel and walked toward the cabin-door. But Richard called her back.

'No, Anna — please — come back!'

There was a note in his voice that stopped her immediately. She turned round to him. Her face softened.

'You want me?'

'Yes, yes, you mustn't go away again — ' he raised himself on his elbow once more. He, too, was shaking. 'My wife has come here entirely against my will. She agreed to stay in 'Frisco. I won't let you go, Anna.'

Madge Strange put her hands in her coat-pockets. Her sharp, cold face was flushed to the roots of the blonde hair.

'Richard!' she said in a furious voice. 'How dare you? Are you intimating that you — you want this young *person* here with you — instead of me?'

'Madge, we agreed to separate,' said

Richard. 'You followed me out here, and — '

'And you'd be a dead man if I hadn't!' she broke in. 'If I hadn't found a guide who had passed you on the trail and knew whereabouts you were and kindly helped me here.'

'I grant you that. I'm very grateful to you for what you've done these last few hours. But you shouldn't have come. The Yukon is not the place for you.'

'This is intolerable,' said Madge. 'We're married and — '

'Wait, Madge,' he broke in. 'You know as well as I do that we've been damned unhappy. At one time I'd have done anything on earth for you. Nothing I wanted more than to be happy with you. You made it impossible. I'm not going into details but you know all about it. You only want me now because I'm through with it — because you've killed my affection for you.'

Madge Strange did not answer for a moment. She stood there, hands clenched at her sides. She knew that he spoke the truth. She *had* denied him everything. His boyish adoration of her; his selfless devotion at the beginning of their marriage had bored her and she had flung it all back at him. She had been selfish and unsympathetic. And today she wanted him, his homage and devotion, again. It was as he said. He had grown tired . . . He treated her now as she had once treated him; coldly and indifferently. She was nearer to feeling passion for him now than she had ever been. Because he wanted to leave her, he had become the one and only man on earth she wanted. She was not going to let anybody else get him. She had never dreamed, for a moment, that he would want to leave her for another woman. It infuriated her to think that he had become intimate with a girl out here in the wilderness of the North. And such a child, Madge thought indignantly; a half-educated little savage in boy's attire. Anna, indeed. How dared Richard call her back and tell her to stay.

'Look here, Richard,' she said through set teeth. 'I decline to discuss our private affairs before this — er — young person. You seem to have grown very familiar with each other. But don't flatter yourself that I shall divorce you — I *never* will!'

'I looked upon divorce as the wrong thing once, Madge,' said Richard. 'But now I want my freedom. I admit freely that I love Joanna Grey.'

'You dare to tell me that!'

'I'm being perfectly straight with you,' he said. 'It's only because I want to be free that you've taken up this attitude. In the old days, day after day, night after night, you left me to go to your bridge and your poker and your music. You didn't care whether I lived or died. Now, because I've found someone who does care . . . someone whose affection is sincere and unselfish — you want me back. I tell you, Madge, it is grossly unfair of you.'

'I don't care. I shall not walk out and hand you to this girl!' said Madge.

Joanna stood by listening to the altercation between husband and wife. It so deeply concerned her own personal happiness. She was baffled. She knew not what to say or do. All her life, if and when she had thought about marriage, she had regarded it as something sacred . . . a complete union of body and mind between a man and a woman. She had told herself that if one took the marriage vows one could never retract or break them.

But the marriage . . . between Richard and Madge . . . how could it be called a true union? It had never been a union at all. Why should Mrs. Strange want to keep her husband now; why in her perverse fashion should she make up her mind to keep him just because he no longer wanted her? Joanna, herself, was so sincere, so full of simplicity that petty spite and perversity were beyond her comprehension.

At the same time, Madge *was* Richard's wife. How could she, Joanna, stay here? What right had she to stay with Richard now that his wife had joined him?

Richard held out a hand to her.

'Anna, I'm so damned sorry about it all . . . it's beastly for you . . . but my dear, my dear, don't go away . . . '

She looked down at him in silence a moment. All the love, the longing in her passionate, honest young heart, lay in her eyes. But she shook her head in a puzzled way.

'Richard, how can I possibly stay now?'

'You must,' he panted. His brow was wet. He was weak and in no fit state to stand an emotional scene. 'You're all alone; you have no one in the world . . . nowhere to go. Anna child you must stay here. Madge . . . ' he appealed to his wife, 'for the moment put aside personal grievances. This girl is only eighteen. Her father died out here the other day. She is alone; in need of protection. Madge — '

'Oh, please, Richard, if you think I

am going to protect your mistress, you're wrong,' broke in Madge.

Joanna turned round. She stared at the older woman. She was trembling.

'Mistress — ' she repeated. 'I — don't understand.'

'Madge, what a damnable thing to say,' said Richard hotly. 'And it isn't true. Can't you see for yourself she's a mere child. Look here — '

She moved to his side.

'Oh, I don't believe in this innocent child business. The girl is obviously in love with you and you're stupidly flattered!'

'Flattered! Good Heavens!' He moved his head impatiently. 'You can't recognise truth when you see and hear it. You never could. Look here, Madge, I ask you to be decent — it is only common decency — not to let this child go out alone — amongst all these rough gold-diggers — it's unthinkable!' He stopped, panting. He was livid.

'Please don't mind about me,' said Joanna. She could scarcely bear to look at him. 'Richard, I don't mind going away. You must see for yourself — I can't stay under these conditions. It would be impossible.'

'Quite,' said Madge.

Joanna gave her a quick, scornful look. She would like to have said much; but she shut her mouth and kept it sealed. For Richard's sake, she was silent. But Madge Strange had insulted her twice; spoken to her as Joanna had never been spoken to before. All that was fierce and wild and proud in her was raw; quivering.

She felt that it would break her heart in two to leave Richard. But she had no other choice. She would have given years off her life to feel his arms about her and his lips upon hers . . . just once more. Why, why was he married to this cold, sarcastic, cruel woman who kept him chained to her just because he wanted to go?

'Oh, Richard,' she whispered forlornly.

'Anna,' he panted. 'Don't . . . don't

go . . . I can't bear it . . . you all alone
. . . little Anna . . . '

He fell back on the pillow; his eyes
closing, his lips blue.

Joanna flung herself down beside
him.

'Richard — Richard — Richard!'

Madge Strange stared down at her
husband. The malicious look on her
face gave place to one of fear.

'Is he dead?' she said.

'No,' said Joanna taking Richard's
hand. 'He's fainted. Have you brandy?'

'Yes, here — ' Madge handed the
younger girl a flask. She was forced to
let Joanna take the lead here. She was
terrified of sickness and death. Illness in
any shape or form had always nause-
ated her and frightened her.

When she had first arrived at this
cabin; she had found it with the aid of a
Sour-dough who knew the country; it
had been first of all a triumph to find
her husband and feel that she had him
chained to her side again; then a worry.
He was a dying man when she got to

him. She was forced to give him brandy; nurse him in her rather helpless, ignorant fashion. She loathed nursing! She could not bear the sight of blood or sickness. She had come out here with her camping-outfit; her snow-boots; her appearance of strength and capability. And under it all she was a silly, squeamish woman; stubborn rather than brave; cowardly behind the superior and censorious attitude which she adopted. She was the type to go to pieces quickly. And she was going to pieces now. To herself she admitted she had had enough of nursing Richard in this isolated cabin which had none of the comforts to which she was used.

She watched angrily while Joanna took off her fur mittens and coat and ministered to Richard. She hated the sight of the girl. Rude, horrible little thing. But she seemed to know what to do for Richard. In a few moments his eyes were open again. His heart was beating more regularly. His pulse was stronger. Joanna gave him sips of brandy and milk. He lay quiet, just looking up at her, with silent gratitude.

'He'll die — he'll die if he stays here,' Madge Strange suddenly burst out in hysterical fashion. 'He ought to be got back to some civilised place. This is what has gone on ever since I arrived — fainting fits — and I don't know what to do.'

Joanna rose to her feet and turned to the elder woman.

'What have you been doing for him?'

'Giving him food. And he's been so sick . . . '

'You mean a lot of food?'

'Yes, he was starving. He needed it.'

Joanna's lips curled. She thought Mrs. Strange a very foolish woman. When a man was starving, a lot of food would make him sick. He was very, very weak. The least excitement would make him faint. He needed careful attention. Just sips of brandy and milk until he was in a condition to take solid food. Joanna had nursed men before . . . friends of her father's. Many half-starving, dying

87

creatures had stumbled into their cabin for help.

She wondered what she ought to do. Whether she ought to leave Richard in the care of this incapable wife of his? Her scornful gaze travelled over Madge's blonde exquisitely coiffed head, her smart coat and boots. Then she said:

'He ought not to have anything but brandy and milk today.'

Madge looked up, then quickly down. She twisted a wet handkerchief in her long white fingers.

'Well, look here. You'd better stay. I — as a matter of fact — I hate sick-beds and I don't understand illness. Besides I haven't got unlimited supplies of food or brandy. I expected to get back to home as soon as I found Richard. What can I do?'

'I can send Kiche, my Indian, for what you need.'

'Then please do,' said Madge.

'I'll go with him,' said Joanna shortly. 'Goodbye.'

'No, don't,' stammered Madge. She

was rapidly climbing down from her perch. 'You — you'd better stay and look . . . help me look after my — my husband.'

'Yes — please — stay,' came Richard's feeble voice.

Then Joanna decided, definitely, that while he was so ill and in need of her, she could not deny him. He had half-killed himself for her. She must stay with him now, even though the presence of this woman, his wife, made the situation intolerable.

'I'll stay,' she said abruptly. 'I'll send Kiche to fetch what stores we shall need.'

6

Evening came.

Kiche, the Indian had not yet come back from Fort Yukon with fresh supplies. Quite possibly he would not be able to get there until tomorrow.

The brief day of sunlight had quickly gone. It was dark and bitterly cold again. The sky was heavy with sinister cloud. A faint, moaning wind sobbed round the little cabin. Joanna with experienced eye, looked out and predicted another storm.

Madge Strange had regained some of her dignity and poise. She allowed Joanna to do the unpleasant jobs, but she stood over her all the time with an eagle-eye and took care that it was she, his wife, who shook up his pillows; smoothed his blankets; brushed his hair. He was restless, almost sullen under her hands. She saw that. And she also saw how his whole face changed when Joanna touched him. A look of passionate love came into his eyes, that Madge had never seen even in the old days.

The atmosphere was a difficult one; charged with hostility between the two women. The one who wanted Richard Strange out of malice and perversity; the other who loved him simply and utterly without one shred of selfishness.

Joanna's one desire was to make him strong and well again. She did all that was necessary for him gladly; with happiness. And when there was nothing to do and he slept . . . she sat in a corner of the cabin and watched him. Madge Strange, too, sat in her corner and watched both of them in a stealthy jealous fashion.

Once, Joanna in her big-hearted, simple fashion, held out a hand to the woman.

'Let us try and be friends,' she said. 'We are forced into this position — to do what we can for him. Let us try to be friends. I've never had an English-woman to talk to, like this — won't you talk to me?'

Madge, instead of responding to the greatness of it, was petty and ungenerous.

'I admit we're forced into the position but I see no reason why we should become friends. In fact every-thing is against it,' she said.

Joanna did not offer her hand again.

Night came. In the little cabin, yellow with the light from the oil-lamp on the table, three people tried to sleep. Richard, now wakeful and restless on his mattress; Madge beside him on the camp bed she had brought for herself; well wrapped in fur-robes and jaegar blankets. Joanna in the opposite corner, curled up in one fur-robe which Madge had offered with icy courtesy.

Richard could not tear his gaze from the small figure of the girl he loved. He felt stronger tonight. His heart beat quickly and painfully as he saw how uncomfortable she was and yet, as usual stoic, uncomplaining. He frankly hated the woman who was his wife; snug and warm on her camp bed. She was the first to sleep. But Richard could not close his eyes and long after the lamp had been extinguished, he lay tossing . . . torn with longing to speak to Joanna . . . intimately, passionately, as they had spoken when they had discovered their love for each other the other night.

He heard her give a little sigh. He whispered her name.

'Anna . . . '

At once she was up and at his side; afraid that he was ill and in need of her. Madge slept soundly, heavily, and did not hear. Joanna bent over Richard.

'You want me?'

'Come . . . closer . . . just a moment, my dear.'

Her face flushed. She knelt down by the mattress. He put out his hands and laid them on her shoulders; looked up through the darkness but could not see her face. Then touched her hair; her cheeks, her eyes with his fingers.

'Oh, little Anna . . . my darling!'

'Oh, hush,' she whispered. 'You mustn't . . .'

'But I love you so! You're uncomfortable; cold, yes, I feel you shaking . . . I can't bear it . . .'

'I'm all right, honestly. Don't worry.'

'I can't bear it,' he repeated. 'The whole position is frightful.'

'I know,' she said forlornly. 'But you're ill and you need me . . . I must stay. When you're better, I'll go.'

'No,' he said under his breath. 'No . . . I can never let you go again . . .'

She tried to draw away from him. The touch of his hands on her hair made the blood race through her veins. She loved this man as she had never loved anybody on earth. She wanted to put her face against his and lie close in his arms . . . close . . . close; to ease the wild aching of her heart. She, usually so strong, was weak under the touch of his hand . . . the sound of his voice.

'Little Anna,' he whispered. 'I can't let you go . . .'

A shiver passed through her. Just for a moment her resistance weakened. She was in his arms; straining close to him. Their lips were one in a kiss that drained her of strength. The embrace seemed to give him new life, new vitality. He held her madly; kissed her again and again. She kissed him back; let her lips linger on his eyelids; against his hair. She wished almost that she could die, there in his arms before that sweet embrace ended.

Then sanity returned to her. She drew away from him and hid her face in her hands.

'We're mad, Richard. Your wife is here. We can't do this!'

He felt weak and spent now that she was gone from him. Immense depression seized him.

'Oh, little Anna . . . forgive me . . .'

'It's as much my fault,' Joanna's voice broke. 'It's so — awfully difficult for us both. But I suppose we must try, Richard . . . '

Madge Strange woke up with a start. She sat up; wide awake in an instant. She struck a match and lit the candle she had put on the floor beside her. She saw Joanna standing beside Richard; Joanna with hot cheeks and tears in her eyes.

'I might have guessed you'd behave like this . . . you little bad lot . . . ' Madge Strange said, 'making love to my husband in the middle of the night when you think I'm asleep.'

'Oh, Madge, for God's sake — ' began Richard.

'I won't have it,' she broke in violently. 'You are my husband and I won't have it — do you hear?'

Joanna put her hands to her ears. She felt as though Madge's violence stifled her. The whole atmosphere stifled her. Richard loved her . . . She loved him. But how could they find happiness in each other. This woman, this wife of his, stood between them. It was a maddening position. She looked at Madge with eyes full of suffering.

'I apologise to you, Mrs. Strange,' she said. 'You have a right to be angry. I am sorry. I — I can promise you it won't happen again.'

'I won't let you apologise,' said Richard. 'My wife is my wife in name only and has been for years. She can't suddenly behave as though she wanted me exclusively for herself. It's ridiculous. As soon as I'm fit enough, Anna, I shall ask you to go away with me.'

'She can go with you with pleasure,' said Madge, lapsing back into cold sarcasm. 'But I shan't divorce you.'

Joanna turned away. She was shivering. She felt that if she remained here in this room — shut up like this with the man she loved and his wife — she would go mad.

'I think — ' began Madge.

Then she stopped. Suddenly the silence of the night was broken by a long, fierce, melancholy cry. A cry that made the blood of those that heard it run cold. It was answered by other cries, howling, hungry sounds. In the candle-light Madge Strange's face went livid.

'What's that?'

'Wolf,' said Joanna briefly.

Madge sprang out of bed, she clutched a blanket around her. Her teeth began to chatter.

'Wolves . . . how ghastly! Will they hurt us?'

Richard also sat up. He looked at Joanna. She showed no sign of fear and his heart exalted. There was something very fine about this slip of a girl, something so steadfast, so brave.

Madge repeated her words.

'Will they hurt us? Joanna . . . you know . . . say something.'

Joanna listened a moment. The cries of wolves were more distinct. She looked quickly round the cabin.

'What ammunition have we?'

'I don't know,' stammered Madge. 'I've g-got a rifle but I'm f-frightened to use it.'

'Give it to me,' said Joanna.

Madge handed her the rifle and some cartridges. Joanna examined it deftly. She was used to rifles. Richard watched her with growing admiration. He said:

'Anna, is there any danger? We're all right in here.'

'Yes. But they're hungry. That's the hunger cry. They'll sit round and worry us a bit. I'll take a few shots from the window.'

Another fierce cry, much more distinct this time made Madge's blood run cold. She sank on her bed in a state of panic.

'Oh, why did I ever come up to this dreadful place? It's terrible . . . I'm so frightened.'

The window-pane rattled. Joanna drew back, she bit her lip.

'That was a wolf,' she said. 'They smell food in here.'

'I must get up — I must do something,' said Richard.

He staggered on to his feet. He was so weak and giddy, and swayed at once. Joanna put the rifle down and hurried to him; supported him in her strong young arms.

'You must lie down at once.'

'But I can't leave you to do everything — a girl — a child.'

'I'm not afraid,' she said. 'I've lived out here most of my life.'

Helplessly, the sick man lay down again. He cursed his own weakness. The cabin was revolving round him. He was too weak to help Joanna. But his manhood revolted from letting her do everything. He could not endure it. He lay gasping, watching her; adoring her. He felt nothing but contempt for his wife. She sat on her bed hysterically sobbing in a frenzy of fear for her own personal safety.

Two gleaming eyes showed in the darkness outside the window pane. Madge screamed. Then silence. Something rustled outside the door. There came a strange sniffing, snorting, under it. Madge licked her dry lips.

'They're here . . . they'll get in . . . we shall all be killed . . . '

'Put out the light,' said Joanna. 'I want to open the window a little and get one of the brutes.'

Madge, frenzied, clutched at the candle.

'No — don't open the window — they'll get in — don't — '

The flame of the candle licked at a trailing flimsy garment on Madge's bed. It was disastrous. The whole bed was set on fire. Joanna dropped the rifle and rushed for water. But there was only half a pailful of snow-water which Kiche had filled for them before he went and not nearly enough to extinguish the blaze. Then, and then only, Joanna knew fear. She looked at Richard with panic in her eyes.

'Now what shall we do? If we open the door, the wolves will get us. If we stay in here we shall be burnt alive. Richard . . . Richard . . . it'll mean death for us . . . either way!'

Madge gave a stifled moan and collapsed on to the floor at Richard's side. She had fainted.

Richard looked at his wife's prostrate form.

'Madge ... Madge ... wake up ... pull yourself together. This isn't the time to faint. Madge, for the love of heaven — wake up — you've got to help Anna.'

Joanna set her teeth.

'We've all got to help ourselves now, Richard. We can't stay in here and get burned alive. We must go out. The fire, for as long as it burns will keep the wolves back. The only thing to do is to keep it burning ... d'you understand? There are some spruce logs ... Kiche cut them for us before he left ... '

She broke off and drew in her breath sharply. A tongue of fire circled round the mattress on which Richard was lying ... the next moment his bed was aflame. He got up; white; tottering; weak. He was a very sick man and unable to help anybody but himself. He cursed his weakness. He said in a hoarse voice:

'Give me the gun, Anna, you must

see to Madge . . . '

Madge recovered consciousness. She sat up and began to shriek and wail when she found herself in the burning cabin. The acrid smell of burning wood soon restored her fully to her senses. The next moment she was on her feet, clinging to the younger girl.

'We shall all be burned . . . oh, help! . . . help!'

'Please be quiet,' said Joanna. 'Screaming won't do any good. There's no one to help us until Kiche comes back. But we've got to keep this shack burning. That is the only way to drive the wolves back.'

She opened the cabin door. A bitterly cold gust of wind swept in, bringing with it a shower of powdered snow from the spruce-trees lying round the cabin. At the same time a she-wolf — a lean, grey, hungry shape — sprang back and stood hesitating, snarling. She had been sniffing under the cabin door. Richard managed somehow to aim and fired. With a howl of pain the she-wolf dropped on her side and died. He had hit her through the head. Now, out of the darkness appeared other lean grey shapes, gleaming eyes, three or four wolves of a pack; sitting on their haunches; watching; waiting.

Joanna took Madge by the arm and pulled her out of the cabin. The woman was so mad with fright that she could scarcely stand. Trembling, shaking at the knees, she leaned against Joanna sobbing hysterically.

'We shall be eaten alive . . . oh, look . . . look!'

Joanna looked . . . not at the wolves, which she knew would keep away so long as the cabin blazed . . . but at Richard. He was ill and unfit to stand out here in the bitter cold with that heavy gun. He was as white as the very snow. But his eyes met and held hers in a long look of passionate admiration.

'You're a brave little thing, Anna,' he said.

Madge was too frenzied with fear to resent that speech. Another wolf, more daring than the rest sprang forward. Madge gave a blood-curdling scream of terror. Joanna opened the cabin door again and a tongue of fire spat out into the darkness followed by a dense cloud of smoke. The wolf retreated and sat down again, whimpering.

The pack was very hungry.

Joanna shivered with cold but she wasted no more time.

'Keep the fire burning and we're all right,' she said. 'If a wolf springs at you, pick up a burning brand and throw it. They won't stand fire.'

'Joanna, come here . . . stay by me,' wailed Madge.

Joanna gave her a look of contempt.

'I can't. There's too much to do. Come round to the back of the cabin and fetch some logs. We must keep this blaze going.'

'I daren't . . . Richard . . . Richard, save me!' said Madge sobbing convulsively.

He did not answer her. He was staring grimly at the pack of wolves

. . . his gun ready. Madge stumbled over the snow to his side and caught at his arm. He shook her off.

'Pull yourself together. Don't be such a coward. Look at that brave child . . . copy her . . . '

Madge looked resentfully at Joanna who had reappeared with an armful of spruce-logs.

'She's used to this sort of thing. I'm not,' she whimpered.

'You must try and help me,' said Joanna. 'This is the only thing to do. We must keep the fire burning until Kiche comes . . . '

And for the next two hours, that was Joanna's sole thought and job. For two solid hours, with the icy wind whistling round them and the hungry wolves circling them . . . that ill-assorted trio stood together; waiting for the Indian to bring relief.

7

The cabin burned merrily. It cast a lurid glow around them. They could see the wolves plainly . . . sitting on their haunches, watching them at a safe distance. Joanna fully realised the fate that might befall them if that fire died down . . . and the pack sprang . . .

Richard had collapsed through sheer weakness. He lay on the snow at Joanna's feet. Joanna stood over him like a little soldier, protecting him; the gun in her hand. She was sick with suspense. There was such horror in the thought that Kiche might not come. Madge clung to her arm; she had done nothing to help; only sobbed and whimpered as the hours dragged by.

They were not so cold now. The conflagration behind them kept them warm and that warmth undoubtedly saved Richard from pneumonia that night. Madge was wrapped in blankets only. Joanna was fully clad. She had not undressed when she had retired for the night.

They were all three desperately tired and worn. They dared not sleep. Dared not relax the awful tension for one single moment. When the little cabin was razed to the ground, they had to pile on spruce-logs and keep the flames fed. And the wolves stayed a few yards away ... watching ... waiting. One began to howl. The others joined. Then the entire pack howled that awful hunger-cry; their noses pointed to the sky.

At the end of the third hour, Madge's feeble strength gave out. She was an arrogant, aggressive woman in her own drawing room in a civilised Western world. Out here in the Yukon, facing such horrors as this, she was a coward. She had none of Joanna's endurance or courage. She sank on to the snow beside her husband and lay there, moaning. Joanna looked down at her, with half-contemptuous pity. Richard stared up at her with his sunken eyes. The red spots showed on his cheeks.

'I must apologise for my wife. It's damnable you should have no help. But I'm afraid Madge hasn't the nerve to stand this,' he said. 'She ought never to have followed me. It was only because she wanted to thwart my wish to be alone and get away from her . . . What a marvellous person you are, little Anna, you haven't turned a hair — you've done everything, saved us all, alone and unaided.'

She gave him a swift, warm look. Her lips quivered.

'I don't feel very marvellous, Richard. To tell you the truth I feel sick with fright.'

'Who would think it, to look at you.'

She stood silent; her large eyes staring through the flame-lit darkness at the wolf-pack; her small body was tense.

'Talk to me, Richard . . . it will help me . . . keep me going.'

'I love you,' he said.

'Don't say that . . . ' her face flushed. 'Your wife is here.'

'She's too damned scared to worry,' he said contemptuously. 'She ought to be at your side, helping you. It makes me sick . . . and I'm a damned weakling.'

'You're ill. It isn't your fault.'

'As long as I live I shall regret being ill just when I should be doing what you've done, little Anna.'

'It's all right, Richard,' she said.

He moved himself over the snow and came nearer her feet. She stooped at once and folded the blankets closer about him.

'Are you warm? Do you get the warmth from the fire?'

'Yes. I'm warm enough — only so damned weak.'

He suddenly caught sight of her hands in the firelight. They were torn, bleeding. There were no more of the spruce-logs Kiche had cut for them and Joanna had torn down branches, bushes, bruised and scratched herself. But she had not complained. Richard felt a lump in his throat. Was there ever such a brave child as Joanna Grey?

'Your hands, your poor little hands,' he said. 'Oh, my dear.'

She tried to hide them from him.

'It's nothing . . . they don't hurt.'

'I can't lie here,' he said angrily. 'I can't.'

He tried to struggle on to his feet but fell back again. Joanna shook her head at him.

'You must. It's no use. You're as weak as a baby. Lie there and keep quiet. I'm all right.'

'You must be done in, child.'

'No. I'm all right,' she repeated.

He watched her, silent, baffled by his weakness. She smiled at him now and again but she kept a steady eye on the pack waiting grimly in the shadows. Madge lay quiet, huddled in her blankets. She had sunk into a kind of stupor.

'Little Anna,' said Richard. 'How

much longer can you stand there, keeping watch?'

'Until Kiche comes, I hope.'

'Be honest with me. Aren't you very done?'

'I'm tired and sleepy. But talk to me. Keep me going. Tell me a joke. Ask me some riddles. Keep me awake.'

'What can I say to you except that I love you and think you're the gamest woman God ever made, Anna.'

'No . . . don't flatter me. Tell me — about England. I used to like it when Daddy told me about England.'

Richard looked up at her. The small stoic figure in the fur coat and breeches stood gallantly there, poised for action, gun in her hands. The firelight played on her face and it seemed to him amazingly noble, even happy. He said huskily:

'England's rather a fine country, little Anna. It breeds folk like you. When you were only a very small child out here, there was a war when Englishmen fought for their Country and went into the trenches and into action with a jest on their lips . . . They showed the sort of spirit you have shown tonight, little Anna.'

'Make me laugh, Richard. Don't make me cry.'

He put an arm about her ankles and kissed her feet.

'I love you — '

'I love you,' she said, and the tears rolled down her cheeks.

Madge Strange opened her eyes and began to moan.

'Richard, where are you? Oh, Richard, hold me . . . come near me. Oh, I'm so cold, I'm so terrified, Richard . . . '

Joanna listened to this until she could not stand it.

'Go to her, Richard,' she said. 'I'm all right. She can't help being frightened, poor thing. And she *is* your wife. Do what you can . . . '

'Generous as well as brave,' said the man, and clung for a moment to her ankles; his face pressed to the small feet that stood there so steadfastly. Then he moved over and over to his wife and put an arm around her shoulders. 'Buck up,' he said with an effort. 'Madge . . . Madge . . . don't give way like this . . . be a sport . . . '

She crawled into his arms, shivering, moaning. Her fair hair was unpinned, falling loosely about her face. Her blue eyes were brilliant with terror.

'Hold me tight . . . hold me . . . Richard . . . Don't let those awful wolves get me. Richard be nice to me again — like you used to be.'

He held her. But there was neither love nor pity in that embrace . . . only a sense of duty. She clung wildly to him. His eyes looked over her head at the girl who was their saviour and without whom they might have died a horrible death tonight. She no longer looked at him. She watched the wolves. Behind them the fire was dying down. There were no more spruce-logs to feed the flames. The brave little figure did not move. But Joanna's eyes were full of an intolerable pain. The thought of death did not worry her. But the thought of life without Richard was worse than death. The woman who huddled in his arms for comfort in this hour was an immovable barrier between them. Joanna felt utterly alone.

Then came the sound of a sled churning over the snow and the eager barking of dogs. Richard looked up at Joanna. New life surged through his numbed body.

'Your Indian, Anna . . . I believe we're saved.'

'Yes, it is Kiche,' she said.

A little sob of sheer exhaustion tore her throat as she saw Kiche coming toward them. But it was drowned in the sound of Madge Strange's shrieks of hysterical delight. The wolf-pack dispersed . . . disappeared into the night. Kiche the Indian drew up his sled and stared at the smouldering ruins of the cabin, a look of profound astonishment on his usually impassive face.

'Yes, it caught fire, Kiche,' said

Joanna. She had dropped the gun and let her whole body relax. She was shuddering with cramp and cold, and reaction from the frightful strain of those hours of suspense. 'You must take us home . . . to our own cabin . . . quickly . . . '

'Yes, little White Lady,' said Kiche. 'And I bring food and medicine.'

Madge Strange dragged herself off the ground and cried without restraint. But Joanna said:

'Richard has fainted. Quickly . . . Kiche . . . help me get Mr. Strange on to the sled. We must take him home . . . at once . . . '

The fire had started after midnight. It was dawn when Kiche the Indian landed Richard, Madge, and Joanna at John Grey's former home.

That lone cabin, in the midst of the white vast wilderness, was like a small dark blot on the immensity of the snow-covered land. The darkness of the heavens was rift by pale grey streaks of light. A sad, mournful light, ghostly, shadowy and uncertain. Richard was half-conscious when Kiche lifted him in his strong arms and bore him inside the cabin. Madge alternately laughed and cried and talked hysterically about nothing. But Joanna was silent. Profoundly depressed, exhausted, she walked into the little house wherein she had lived for so long with her father and thought of the old days and of him. The days that were no more. Everything was changed.

In a measure this sitting room was the same. The bedroom, the kitchenette; the faded blue curtains; the stained strips of carpet; her father's old rocking-chair; her own favourite stool; everything unchanged. But he was gone. Therefore this home from which she had fled in fear and loathing of Conrad Owen was Home no longer.

Outside, pathetic and small in the grey light of the frozen dawn, a small white cross marked the grave in which Kiche and the priest had laid John Grey to his last long rest. Joanna had passed it as she entered the cabin. Passed

. . . not daring to pause a moment in case she broke down and sobbed. And she must not break down. There was still so much to be done. Richard was ill. Exhausted though she was, Joanna wanted to give him her attention. Madge was worse than useless.

With a great effort, Joanna steeled herself against the desire to drop down in a heap on the floor and sleep. She told Kiche to light the stove and bring wood and snow-water. He carried out her orders obediently. He brought in the food and medicines which had come from Fort Yukon.

Madge Strange sat down and watched, staring curiously around her. This was a much larger, more habitable cabin than that other awful little shanty had been, she thought. And this was Joanna Grey's home. With cold curiosity, Madge stared at the one or two dilapidated cushions in the chairs; the photographs and pictures on the walls; the needlework basket on the table beside the lamp. The newspapers and tattered magazines . . . all a year or two old . . . the chipped, common crockery and glass. Joanna's house.

Richard was making a fool of himself over a girl with such an outlandish, primitive home; no education, no culture.

Madge had recovered from her hysteria and fright. She was cool and herself again. She decided to get Richard home to England with her at once. She was not going to let him stay out here with Joanna Grey. She would ask him to begin again — to be as happy as he had first been with her in Ceylon.

Richard lay on the couch drawn up to the stove which the Indian had lighted. His eyes were closed. His handsome sunken face was at peace. He was sleeping. The warmth of the fire and the delicious comfort of the cabin had done their work. Joanna covered him with the fur-robe which had belonged to her father. It was bitter-sweet for her to see Richard on that couch, Daddy's couch . . . and to have

119

him here in her old home — Richard whom she loved. Bitter-sweet to have him here for a little while. It would only be for a while. When he was strong and well again, the woman who was his wife would take him away. Joanna knew she must urge him to go. He was married and had a contract to carry out, and she had no right to keep him when he belonged to Madge.

An almost fierce resentment against life ached in her heart as she looked down at the sleeping man. Why, why did he belong to Madge? What right had Madge Strange to stand between them?

Madge's voice broke in upon her reflections.

'Do you think that my husband will be all right? He won't develop pneumonia or something dreadful?'

'I hope not; I think, with rest and care he will be all right. When he wakes, we will give him some milk and brandy. Kiche has brought calves-foot and Brand's essence. Gradually he should get back his strength.'

Madge shivered.

'This place is certainly more substantially built than the other awful hole. The wolves can't get in, can they?'

'No,' said Joanna abruptly.

Then she looked straight at Richard's wife:

'We must be very careful of candles and lamps — please.'

'Oh, very well,' said Madge sullenly. 'But don't blame me for the affair in that shanty. The whole business began through your disgraceful behaviour with my husband in the middle of the night.'

Joanna flushed from chin to brow.

'I'm very sorry . . . '

'The whole affair's a disgrace,' added Madge. 'And the sooner you realise that Richard is my husband, the better.'

'I think I do realise it, Mrs. Strange,' said Joanna. 'Please don't let's quarrel over him. I'm — nearly done in. Do you mind if I snatch an hour's sleep? Would you watch by Richard? When he wakes, give him milk and brandy. I'll let you have a rug and a cushion. The rocking-chair is very comfortable.'

'But I must lie down. I'm tired out. I can't start sick nursing,' said Madge.

Joanna's lips twisted. Her dark, sad eyes were red-rimmed with fatigue. Her face was white.

'Mrs. Strange, I didn't relax my attention for hours out there. I'm not grumbling, but I *must* rest or I shall collapse. I'm afraid there is only one bed in the little room through that door . . . my old room. My father used to have the couch. You can have the bed for the rest of the day when I've snatched half an hour's sleep.'

'Why can't your Indian servant watch Richard? I am utterly exhausted,' said Madge.

Joanna stared at her.

This incredibly selfish woman said she loved and wanted her husband back. And she couldn't watch him . . . look after him . . . for an hour?

Joanna turned to Kiche who was

unpacking tins of food in the kitchenette.

'Kiche, watch by the white master
and call me when he wakes,' she said
briefly. Then to Madge: 'Will you come
this way, Mrs. Strange.'

Madge followed the slim boyish
figure. Joanna made her feel ashamed.
She loathed the girl.

Joanna pointed to a camp bed in the
tiny room which had been hers for so
many years. Not uncomfortable, with
its combination-dressing-table and wash-
stand and strip of carpet. There were
blankets and sheets on the bed. A few
clothes hung from wooden pegs in a
corner-cupboard behind a faded cre-
tonne curtain. It looked lovely — heaven
— after the rough shanty from which
they had come. A haven of rest and
peace after the night of horror in the
snow.

Joanna left Madge to undress and lie
down in the bed. Then she returned to
the living room and wrapped herself in
a blanket and sat in her father's

rocking-chair. It was Kiche, the Indian, who with brown hands as tender as a woman's, put a cushion at his little White Lady's head. Kiche who covered her feet with a fur-robe. Joanna gave one last look at Richard, then, satisfied that he slept peacefully; shut her eyes. She was dead tired. In two minutes she was sound asleep.

She awoke to feel Kiche gently shaking her.

'Little Lady . . . master awake . . . little Lady . . . wake up . . . '

Joanna had slept for a couple of hours. She was still very tired. She had to drag herself back to consciousness. When she realised what Kiche was saying, she opened her sore eyes and hurried to Richard's side.

'Other white lady, she sound asleep,' said Kiche.

'Very well,' said Joanna tersely. 'Heat some milk Kiche and bring it to me.'

The Indian departed. Joanna stood by Richard's couch. She was wide awake now. He, too, was awake. He was very weak but he held out a hand, dumbly, and she took it and held it tightly between her strong young fingers. The day was here; a brief, grey, sunless day. The skies were still lowering; heavy with snow-clouds. Everything looked grim and lifeless. And in the grim light, Richard Strange's face looked to Joanna much too thin and white.

'My darling . . . ' before she could restrain the words, she said them, huskily. The child, the girl, was mother as well as lover. And sorrow and hardship had aged her during the last few terrible weeks. 'Are you better?'

'Yes, Anna, I had a wonderful sleep. And you . . . my poor little girl?'

'I've had a wonderful sleep, too. I'm fit and fine.'

He could see plainly, however, that the strain had bitten deep into her small, pale face. He who loved her was not deceived.

'You're worn out, Anna. Why didn't you go on sleeping?'

She did not tell him that she had

ordered Kiche to rouse her. She smiled and said:

'I woke up. Now, Richard . . . some hot milk and brandy. We must feed you and get you strong again.'

'Yes, for God's sake, get me strong. I can't stand lying down and watching you do all the work much longer. Where is *she*?'

'Asleep in my bedroom.'

'She would be,' said Richard. 'It makes me sick . . . you doing everything, like you did last night. Feeding that fire . . . keeping off the wolves. Little Anna, you were so splendid.'

'Oh, rot,' she said boyishly. 'Stop talking and eat . . . '

She made him sip the hot drink. She was rewarded when a tinge of colour came back into his sunken cheeks. When he had drunk the last drop she told him to sleep again. He clung to her hand.

'I don't want to let you go, little darling Anna.'

'But I must,' she said. 'I don't know

126

what the end of this will be. You're married, and — '

'And I have only the most profound contempt for a woman who behaves as she behaved last night,' he broke in. 'And when I'm well you must come away with me. You must, my dear.'

He held her hand to his dry, feverish lips . . . kissed her wrist. She trembled and was weak. She, who was strong in all other things could not be strong when this man whom she loved touched her, kissed her. Her heart ached with desperate need of him.

'Please don't,' she whispered.

'Anna, kiss me.'

'No, I daren't.'

He gave a long sigh and let go her hand.

'Perhaps not. Perhaps you are right. For now. But when I'm well . . . '

'Even then, we mustn't. You must go away and take *her* with you.'

'Never. I will never leave you, beloved little Anna.'

'You must,' she said. 'We neither of

us believe in divorce, in breaking the marriage contract. We would never find happiness that way.'

'Anna, are we to let her stand between us always?'

'Hush . . . you must keep quiet and sleep or you will never get well. We'll talk it out when you are better.'

Impulsively she bent and kissed his forehead. But he dragged her face close to his and for a moment they lay in each other's arms. Cheek pressed to cheek, hearts aching, bursting. He kissed her twice, lingeringly, on the lips. Then she fled from him her eyes blind with tears. She went back to her chair and turned her face to the cushion. She wanted Richard Strange with body, heart and soul, with all the fervent youth of her. She wondered how she could ever exist without him. And yet . . . while that woman who slept so calmly and selfishly, in the next room, existed, Richard could never belong to her, Joanna. It was a tragedy.

8

For another week, Richard Strange and his wife and Joanna lived together in that snow-bound cabin of the frozen Wild.

It was a position of acute embarrassment for them all. Richard grew stronger every day. Between them Joanna and Kiche nursed him back to life. At the end of that week he was up and able to walk about again. A thin shadow of the Richard whom Joanna had first met. But Richard well on the road to health and strength once more.

His love for Joanna increased with every passing day. The position became intolerable. He hardly dared look at Joanna. The presence of Madge made things insupportable. She never left them alone, never let them go out of the cabin for a single minute without following them. She seemed to take a special delight in tormenting them. Really she deceived herself into thinking she was in love with her husband again and willing to start a happily-married life. But her sensations were born of jealousy and the perverse desire to keep Richard against his will.

Day after day; night after night, they sat together, those three, trying to converse. Richard, sullen, wanting only to be alone with Joanna. Madge, watchful; spiteful; never losing an opportunity to throw it down Joanna's throat that she was a 'little savage' totally unfit to take up life in the civilised West. Joanna remained quiet, patient, enduring the jibes and sneers of Richard's wife because she felt guilty of loving Richard. And the pain in her heart ached without ceasing.

Once or twice she tried to get away; to leave the husband and wife alone. But Richard would not let her go. He was still too weak for a long journey and he told Joanna that if she went, he would go, too. She dared not risk him keeping his word. It might mean his death.

But they could not continue like this. One or the other of them would break.

Then two important things happened. Food began to run scarce again. Kiche was sent back to Fort Yukon to get fresh supplies. And Kiche did not come back. What had happened to the faithful Indian, they could not think. Joanna could only suppose he had met with some fatal accident. And, apart from her sorrow for the loyal servant, their position threatened to be a dangerous one. They had no sled; no dogs; no way of obtaining supplies. The food they had could not last for longer than a week or ten days between three of them.

Then, soon after Kiche's departure Madge Strange fell ill. This time it was neither hysteria nor cowardice. She had a definite pain and she was very sick all night. Joanna who attended to her told Richard that she thought his wife had appendicitis.

'Oh lord,' groaned Richard. 'What the devil are we going to do?'

'We can't do anything,' she said. 'Except pray that someone will pass by and take her back to Fort Yukon. There is a doctor there and some sort of chance for her.'

'Poor Madge,' said Richard.

He did not care for her. He could feel nothing but resentment against her because she stood between him and Joanna. But she was ill and it was not in Richard's nature to be otherwise than kind to a sick woman.

Madge lay on the couch, groaning. Her face framed in long fair plaits looked pinched and white. But even in her pain she was malicious.

'What are you two whispering about?' she asked fretfully.

'We were talking of you, Madge,' said Richard.

'Hoping I'll die, I suppose,' she said.

'Oh, no, no — how can you!' exclaimed Joanna, her face burning red. 'How can you think such a thing?'

'Perhaps I will die. I've got such a bad pain. Oh, come and hold my hand,' whispered Madge.

Obediently Richard took a chair beside her. He held her hand and she clung to it with hot, dry fingers. His heart was heavy within him. His eyes followed Joanna's little figure as she went into the kitchenette to prepare some hot milk for Madge. Joanna never thought of herself. Always for others. She was incapable of an ignoble feeling, he thought. But what would happen to them all now? If only Kiche would come back.

Kiche did not come.

They went through another day and night of anxiety and difficulty. Madge grew worse. They could do little for her. Joanna was awake all night, nursing her with as much tenderness as she would have shown her greatest friend.

Just as daylight was fading that next afternoon, and a few great flakes of snow were beginning to whirl through the gloom, heralding a fresh blizzard, a party of men with two sleds, passed by John Grey's cabin. In this party was an American doctor. They were all on their way to Fort Yukon. Richard stopped them and asked them for help. The doctor examined Madge and was sympathetic in a brief fashion but out there in the frozen North the law was 'each man for himself' and the party were chafing to get ahead before total darkness eclipsed the landscape and the blizzard descended on them. The doctor's diagnosis coincided with what Joanna had thought. Appendicitis.

'I don't think it is an acute case so far as I can tell,' he told Richard and Joanna. 'I mean she's not in a dying condition. But I think the appendix ought to come out, and she ought to be seen to at once. There's room for one and one only on my sled. I'll take her on to Fort Yukon.'

Madge heard these words and began to cry.

'I won't leave my husband. He

mustn't stay here alone with this girl. It's not right.'

The doctor stared at Richard and Joanna, who blushed bright red. Then he turned to Madge.

'Say, you're asking for death,' he said bluntly. 'You'd best come along with me.'

'Yes, you must go, Madge,' said Richard. Then added tersely: 'I'll come, too.'

'You can't,' said the doctor. 'There's no room.'

'And none of us will get to Fort Yukon tonight if we don't hurry. The blizzard is coming,' put in one of the other men impatiently.

In the end Madge was carried to the doctor's sled and laid gently on cushions and covered with furs. She wept violently. She was not so afraid of her own physical condition as of leaving her husband and Joanna alone. That seemed to drive her frantic with jealousy and spite. Her last words were:

'Give me your word you'll be faithful

to me, Richard . . . your word . . . I may die . . . you must swear . . . you must!' Her voice rose above the howl of the icy wind.

Joanna sick at heart and hating the whole situation bent over the sick woman.

'Don't worry, please, Mrs. Strange. I'll give you *my* word.'

'And mine,' added Richard. He had no other choice.

The doctor shouted to them as he drove past.

'We'll send you supplies from the Fort. Don't lose heart, and come on to us as soon as you can. I'll look after your wife.'

Then they were gone.

Richard and Joanna, white with snow, walked slowly back to the cabin, and shut the door. Shut out the sound of the wind, the bitter cold, and were secure and warm in the fire-lit cabin. With care they had enough food and fuel to see them through for a fortnight now that there were only two of them.

That meant they would be all right, even if poor Kiche failed to return, until the weather cleared. Then they could go on the trail, on foot to Fort Yukon.

They faced each other in the yellow light. Alone for the first time for many long, heartbreaking days. Nothing to prevent them rushing into each other's arms . . . except their word of honour given to the woman who had gone.

Richard clenched his hands at his sides as he looked at Joanna. She was not the boyish Joanna tonight in fur coat and breeches. She was just a forlorn girl with tired eyes, and drooping shoulders, weary, in a blue check apron over a woollen dress.

She looked steadily at him. She felt an intolerable longing to run into his arms. But she turned away from him.

'Joanna — my dear!'

'Let's get supper, Richard — we've given our word . . . to *her* . . . ' she broke in.

'I know,' he said. 'But I love you. I want you. Anna, it's damnable. Why did

137

she make us promise?'

'Because she knows we love each other. She wanted to be sure we'd play the game. She was right.'

He took a step toward her.

'Anna, you're loyal and great — really great. But I'm weak and tired of trying to play the game. It's an unfair game — Madge knew it.'

'Richard, we must keep our word,' said Joanna. 'Richard, you must help me to be good otherwise I shall let you make love to me and that would end everything.'

'End the agony, which seems to me futile and unnecessary.'

She turned and looked at him again.

'Do you think I couldn't very easily pitch myself into your arms? I'm longing to.'

'Oh, damn it all,' he said miserably.

'I agree,' said Joanna. She was white but smiling, tight-lipped as a boy. 'It's sheer torture. Richard, do you think I'm a fool to mind about honour and that sort of thing? I'm not a prude. I mean, if you weren't married, what would it matter? We're here together and life out here is short, and death is long — why not take our happiness with both hands. I'd be glad to. I've known so little. But you're not free.'

'No, I'm tied, hand and foot,' he said in a hard bitter voice. 'You're quite right, Anna. Everything you say is right. Fancy a child like you commanding a situation like this. It's amazing — you make me ashamed of myself.'

'Oh, Richard, no!'

'Yes,' he said. 'You may have had very little education. My charming wife has called you a little savage of the wilds. But your father brought you up with a sense of right and wrong as well as to be the gamest girl I've ever met — God knows!'

She flushed painfully and fingered a corner of her apron. She felt suddenly shy of the man and the praise. And she knew that she was weak and very unhappy; ready to break at a touch from him if he but knew it.

'I don't know, Richard,' she said, 'but Daddy used to say the thing that mattered most in life was self-control, and if one practised that, the rest of the virtues would naturally follow.'

'He was very right,' said Richard.

'But all the same I do love you — terribly,' she added.

He gave her a long, yearning look. Then turned away from her. He couldn't trust himself to look too long at that brave little figure in the blue check overall; at the small, brave face, the grave brown eyes. Joanna loved him just as much as he loved her. And for the moment she was stronger.

He neither touched her nor attempted to break down the barrier of her strength which was, after all, so frail and easily snapped. He lit the oil-lamp and set it on the table.

'Don't worry,' he said. 'I'll — be good. But I can't promise to help you, Anna. It's all I can do to help myself — tonight.'

The colour stung her cheeks. She

relaxed and moved toward the kitchen-ette.

'I'll get supper,' she said.

She was tired and miserable. The promise that Madge Strange had extracted from them had put a gulf between them. A gulf of honour. What is honour but a sense of loyalty to truth and morality? The mere feeling in one's mind that one should do the right thing. A gulf that can be bridged in the twinkling of a second. Joanna realised how terribly easy it would be to bridge it. She loved this man and he wanted her. They were aching . . . breaking . . . for the close touch of hands and lips . . . for the flaming rapture of an embrace. They were alone and there were no jealous eyes to pry; no acid, spiteful voice to divide them. Nothing but that slender word of honour . . . that frail division.

She felt nervy, uneasy, as she set a pot of rabbit broth to stew on the oil-cooker. She busied herself with preparations for their supper. Did the work gladly. Anything to occupy her thoughts and keep them from dwelling upon the man in the next room. But it was impossible to stop thinking. He was there. She could see him pacing up and down the living room, an empty pipe between his teeth. Even the solace of tobacco was denied him. He had none left. Not a cigarette in the cabin.

Up and down paced Richard; brows fiercely knit; hands locked behind him. Supremely conscious of the girl who was cooking the supper and avoiding him. Supremely conscious of the longing to take her in his arms and bury his lips in her hair.

He tried hard to concentrate on the thought of his wife. She had appendicitis. She was being driven through the frozen, stormy night to Fort Yukon and might never reach there alive. She was his wife. Once he had loved her. Once that long pale face of hers; now so bitter and hard; had been the face of his first love. He had loved her . . . he had buried his lips in her hair; her long blonde hair, so utterly different to Joanna's cropped curls. Different in every way, those two. One, the conventional product of a civilised town; a cold, malicious woman. The other a child of the primitive North; fearless; half-boy; yet warm, passionate woman who would love as she did all other things — generously.

How could he dwell on the thought of Madge? She had killed his love. Destroyed his illusions. Refused him love and children. How could he think of any woman except Joanna who had brought back his ideals and made life beautiful and worth living again?

He covered his eyes with the back of one hand. Oh, this need for the touch of her arms and lips! This tearing need of her!

When she came into the living room with their supper, like a small, silent ghost, he gave her one swift glance . . . then looked away again. Joanna returned the gaze almost shyly. She set the soup on the table and sat down opposite him.

It was not a happy meal. The former spirit of camaraderie had gone; driven away by the fierce feeling of passion which consumed them both. They were striving to remember the woman who stood between . . . whom they could almost feel was there, with them, mocking them, saying:

'You've given your word . . . you can't break it. You daren't.'

Madge was the unwelcome guest at that supper . . . the shadowy third. Richard and Joanna ate their meal in silence. The atmosphere throbbed with unspoken words . . . with repression.

Joanna was the first to break the silence.

'It's snowing now,' she said. 'Can you hear it against the window pane, Richard?'

'Yes,' he said. 'Another blizzard has set in.'

'The second one we've been through together,' she said.

'Yes,' he gave a curt laugh, pushed back his wooden chair and began to pace restlessly up and down. 'But this time we've plenty of food. Enough to last us till the blizzard stops.'

'That's a blessing,' said Joanna.

'But it isn't a blessing, being shut up here together and feeling *her* between us, all the time,' he broke out fiercely. 'It's awful!'

'I know,' Joanna bent her head. 'But we . . . we must . . . try . . . '

'Quite so. I've spent my life trying to do the things I don't want to do and vice-versa, and I daresay you have, too. Anna, little Anna, I've had hell in my life and you haven't known much happiness in yours. Now we've found each other, it's devilish hard that we can't just — be happy.'

She covered her face with her hands.

'It is — hard, Richard. But it must be hard for her, too . . . to have gone away like that, in pain . . . leaving us together . . . when she was so jealous . . . '

'Oh, why should I be sorry for her

jealousy?' he broke out. 'She didn't want me in the old days at home. She laughed at my efforts to make a decent thing out of our marriage . . . my desire to have a kid. She saw nothing but ugliness in passion and lack of breeding in sincerity and truth. Now, after six years she realises she has lost me and that you are everything on earth, and she wants me again. Sheer perversity. I can't — I won't pity her!'

'But her illness.'

'I'm sorry she's ill. Little Anna, you're very sweet to think of her at all.'

Joanna lifted her face to him.

'I love you. I can't help pitying the other woman — who has been foolish enough to lose you.'

'She wouldn't have lost me, Anna, if she had been decent to me — ordinarily decent.'

'I believe that,' she nodded, 'and it may be wicked of me — but I'm glad it's me you love, Richard.'

'Does it mean so much?' he asked. He leaned his hands on the table and stared across at her. She looked at the thin brown face, noticed what deep lines repression had cut across the firm lips; saw what a strain the years with Madge had put upon him.

'It means everything,' she said. 'But don't . . . don't make me weaken. I'm trying so hard to be good.'

He turned from her.

'Anna, it's more than flesh and blood can stand,' he said hoarsely.

She got up.

'Let's try to be happy, to be pals, Richard. We must get through things somehow. Come and help me wash-up . . . all the crockery . . . two bowls . . . two spoons . . . ' she made a gallant effort to joke.

He went with her into the kitchenette.

'You're adorable,' he said. 'There isn't anybody in the world to touch you, Anna.'

They washed up, joking.

But an hour later, when it was time to sleep, the torment began again

. . . that torment of longing for each other. And the *feeling* that Richard's wife was there . . . holding them to their word.

Honour! Honour! The word danced before Richard Strange's vision; jeered at him.

The storm increased in violence as the evening went by. Inside the little cabin it was warm and comfortable. The yellow flicker of the lamp dispelled the gloom. But the wind howled dismally round the cabin as though all the demons of the nether regions were let loose. The snow whirled and spattered against the window. Sometimes, when there was a lull in the storm they could hear the long-drawn, mournful hunger-cry of a wolf.

Joanna found herself growing more and more uncertain of herself. She wanted to throw herself into Richard's arms and lay her head on his breast. If only for a little while . . . what heaven it would be. This lonely cabin in the desolation of the North would become paradise and she would ask no more of life than that . . .

But she dared not go to him; dared not lay one finger on his arm, lest the torch of their mutual passion should blaze into an enduring flame. Then there would be no drawing back . . . nothing, in the future, but regret . . . because they had given their word and broken it.

Joanna held out a hand before she retired to her tiny bedroom and left Richard to the couch in the living room which Madge had vacated.

'Goodnight,' she said, but dropped her hand quickly as though she dared not let him take it.

He saluted her, like a soldier.

'Goodnight, little Anna.'

'Let's hope the roof doesn't blow in. The wind sounds frightful,' she added.

'If it blows in, we'll blow out,' said Richard.

Joking wretchedly, they separated. Joanna shut the door of her bedroom and flung herself down on her bed and buried her face in the pillow so that Richard should not know that she was crying.

9

At midnight Joanna woke up to hear someone calling her name; somebody banging on her door.

'Anna — Anna — Joanna!'

She sat up; rubbed her eyes; and the next moment was out of bed, calling back; wide awake.

'Richard, hello! yes?'

'Come quickly,' he said. 'The roof's leaking in the kitchenette. I think the gale has torn down a couple of logs. You must help me mend it if you don't mind, old thing, or all the food will be swamped. It's snowing like Hades.'

'I'll come,' she said.

Shivering with cold, she lit a candle and flung a coat over her pyjamas and put on a pair of shoes. The next moment she was in the kitchenette with Richard. He, too, wore a coat over his pyjamas. Their gaze met for an instant,

Richard's heart missed a beat when he looked at her, at the sweetness of her face, flushed from sleep; dark curls ruffled over her head, like a child's; and boyish pink and white striped pyjama legs showing below the fur coat. Then he turned his attention to the roof. Snow was pouring in and forming an icy pool on the floor.

'I'll get hold of a board or two — I can break up a board off a packing case, if you'll find nails and hammer, child,' he said.

'Right,' said Joanna.

Soon they were working hard to repair their roof. It was vitally necessary to save their valuable food.

Richard, with Joanna's assistance, stopped the leakage and did what was necessary. It took about twenty minutes. But at the end of it, they were both half-frozen and shivering. The night was bitter. The wind seemed to howl through every crack and crevice. They could hear the blizzard raging violently round the little cabin like a monster waiting to devour them.

When the job was done Richard lit the lamp in the living room.

'You must heat some coffee, darling. You're frightfully cold,' he said, with a brief glance at her pinched little face.

The word 'darling' brought more colour, more warmth back into her face than the coffee could have done. She laughed and suddenly became embarrassingly aware of her pyjamas. The short fur coat only reached her knees. She bent over the oil-cooker and set a pot of coffee to boil.

Her fingers shook so that she spilt some of the boiling liquid as she took the tin pot off the flame.

Richard did not hear her cry of pain. But he saw that she limped when she came into the living room. She held the coffee in one hand and with the other clutched her coat about her shivering body. She set the pot on the table.

'What's wrong, Anna?' he asked.

'Nothing,' she said.

'You're limping.'

'I spilt some hot coffee. Stupid of me.'

'Stupid, indeed. Why, you poor old thing!' he said.

He walked up to her and knelt down at her feet. There was a red inflamed patch on the instep of one small white foot. Such a slim soft foot. It was only the length of Richard's hand. He could not control the impulse to bend and kiss it once. Then he covered it with kisses.

'Don't — ' she said in a smothered voice.

But the thing was done now. With all the will in the world the man could not keep up the pretence of platonic friendship. He sprang up and caught her in his arms. He held her tightly in speechless passion, as though he could never let her go. Just once, her faint voice whispered:

'Richard . . . we mustn't . . . our promise . . . '

Then she, too, was lost. She shuddered in ecstasy and relaxed in his arms. She felt the burning pressure of his lips against her mouth.

Time and space; the bitter fury of the blizzard outside; the word of honour Madge Strange had wrung from them, were obliterated. They clung together in that close and speechless embrace, spent, helpless, like drowning people who have come up from the depths and can breathe again.

His kisses fell hotly upon her lips; her eyes; her hair. She shut her eyes and her arms were locked about his neck. She half fainted in the ecstasy of such loving. Life had nothing more supreme to offer her than this. The mutual passion seemed to her more than earthly. It became, to her young fervent imagination, immortal. Slowly her eyes opened. She put her hands on his shoulders and looked up at him in a vague, dazed way.

'Richard, it's all wrong.'

'I know, darling. But I can't stand it. I honestly can't,' he said. 'Little Anna . . . my little darling . . . we can't go on like this.'

'I know, Richard. But if we break our word to — to Mrs. Strange, won't we regret it all our lives?' she said. She hid her face against his arm. 'Richard . . . listen . . . don't kiss me any more or I can't talk to you.'

'I don't want you to talk. I just want you to kiss me, Anna.'

'You don't,' she said. 'You'd be sorry and you would make me sorry, too, if we don't keep our heads. We've been mad enough, surely.'

The man gave a great sigh. He closed his eyes — battled with himself for a moment and then stood before her, arms hanging at his sides. He lifted one of her little hands to his lips.

'Anna, you'd make any man hate himself. I know you're right . . . '

'It isn't that I don't adore you,' she said. 'If I die tomorrow, I shall feel I've seen the stars and the sun and the moon . . . and all the glories of the earth. I felt that when you held me . . . kissed me . . . just now.'

'You're lovelier than the stars and the sun and the moon,' he said. 'You're like a flame in my arms, little Anna; so much fire, so much courage. Anna you're a born lover, my dear.'

'Am I? It's you who've taught me, Richard. I've never kissed any other man but you,' she said, in her grave simple way.

He looked at her through half-shut eyes. Adorable Anna — with her passion, her generosity and the white innocence of her. Sudden tenderness almost without passion came over him. He picked her up in his arms and held her as though she were a baby. He put his lips against her head.

'Dear little Anna,' he said. 'I'm not fit to kiss your feet, and you ought to have learned about love from a much better fellow than I am. But I do love you and my life belongs to you from now onward. Something must happen. I must be free so that I can marry you. Would you like to marry me, Anna?'

'Yes, terribly, Richard.'

'We'll keep our promise to Madge, Anna,' he went on. 'You're right. We'd hate it if we didn't. I'm damn sorry, sweetheart, I lost my head.'

'I lost mine, too,' she said, hiding her face against his shoulder.

'Adorable little head,' he said, but gently, and held her now, very gently, brushing her hair with his lips.

He sat down in the old-fashioned rocking-chair and drew her on to his knee. She put her head on his shoulder, her arms about his neck, and pressed her cheek against his. He rocked to and fro as though he were holding a small child. They were both very silent and thoughtful for a long while.

Then a big tear forced its way between her closed lids and rolled down her cheek. He felt it, warm and wet against his. He said huskily:

'Oh, my little Anna, don't cry. Something will happen to put things right. Something must happen, for all our sakes.'

He kissed the tears away; and lifted her up and carried her to her room. He laid her on the bed and covered her with the blankets.

'You're shivering so, little love. You must keep warm. I'll bring you your cup of coffee. First I must heat it up. We let it get cold.'

He brought her the hot coffee and stood over her while she drank it. He was dear and gentle and charming to her . . . as though offering a silent apology for that moment of uncontrolled emotion. He knelt down by the bed and kissed her; kissed the blue shadows in the curve of her arm.

'Goodnight, little Anna,' he said. 'Thank you for loving me. God knows it makes me proud. You're brave about everything — love included. And that isn't very easy. Goodnight.'

After he had left her, Joanna lay awake for a long time listening to the fury of the storm, and she felt that her heart was breaking.

Neither of them slept until the grey dawn came up over the desolate country.

Another day commenced.

10

For two days and nights which seemed endless and exhausting, these two who loved each other remained in the snow-bound cabin. And their word to Madge remained unbroken.

The shadowy third was ever with them . . . but each wondered, deep down in their hearts, how long it would be before endurance snapped and their mutual passion sent them into each other's arms.

It was dreary; monotonous in the cabin. The snow never ceased to swirl and fall. Grey, blinding flakes through the gloom of the short day and the inky blackness of the long, bitter night. If they could have clasped hands . . . touched lips . . . felt free to live and love with the incomparable flame of youth . . . the time would have flown by. But they sat apart;

scarcely daring to look at each other; never, after that one tempestuous scene at midnight, losing control.

They spoke incessantly of Madge . . . as though seeking to keep the flag of honour painted in bright colours before them. They wondered how she was; if she had survived the terrible journey to Fort Yukon. If the doctor had operated successfully or otherwise. And they spoke of Kiche, the faithful Indian . . . what had happened to him? Joanna grieved over the mysterious disappearance of Kiche. He had been her servant since her babyhood . . . she mourned him like an old friend.

Then — on the morning of the fourth day — the blizzard ceased. The snow lay thick, crisp, stainless over the wilderness and powdered every spruce tree in the frowning forest. But the sky cleared and a pallid beam of sunshine forced its way through the clouds and turned the country into a glittering panorama. The whole world outside Joanna's little cabin looked as though it were encrusted with diamonds.

Being able to get out relieved the tension of things a little. They put on snow-shoes and swept away the drifts from door and window. Richard went out with his gun to look for a rabbit to give them a hot meal.

Then, suddenly, at midday, Kiche came back. He looked ill and limped badly. But his impassive face was unaltered. When Joanna ran to greet him joyfully, he saluted her in his respectful fashion and gave her a long explanation of his absence. He had been on his way back with fresh supplies and had fallen into the hands of a rough crowd of fur-traders. They had stolen his supplies and commandeered his sled and dogs. Left him to die on the frozen waterway.

By a miracle, before he starved, he was picked up by other traders, less unprincipled, who took him on to Fort Yukon, where he secured fresh supplies and another team of dogs. He made himself a sled of birch-bark and here he was ready to do his White Lady's bidding.

'I am glad, glad you are all right, Kiche,' said Joanna. 'And you come from the Fort? Can you tell us how the other white lady is ... Mr. Strange's wife who was taken away from us, ill?'

'Yes,' said Richard, with a hand on Joanna's shoulder. 'Can you tell us, Kiche?'

The Indian said that he could give them news. They dared not exchange looks — hardly dared breathe as they waited for him to speak. He told them that it was said, in the Fort, that the white lady was so ill, she would not live.

'More than that,' said Kiche gravely, 'the great white doctor bade me tell the Englishman to go straight away to Fort Yukon if he wished to see his wife alive again.'

Richard bit his lip.

'Poor old Madge,' he said. 'Poor Madge, what a position.'

'Richard, of course you must go — immediately,' said Joanna. 'There can be no question about it.'

He gave her a long look. Then he sighed and nodded his head.

'Yes, I must go. But to leave you alone . . . '

'I have Kiche again.'

'Yes, but I dread leaving you, my dear.'

'One day . . . you may come back,' she said. And even he who knew and loved her could not see the agony of anxiety behind her quiet words.

'I must — I will,' he said.

'If your wife is very ill and needs you, you must not leave her, Richard.'

Neither could put into words what might happen either if Madge Strange lived . . . or if she died. They were silent and heavy-hearted. Richard put on his fur coat and cap and mittens; and bade Kiche put the team in the sled for him.

Joanna was dumb, deeply depressed, when the moment came for her to say farewell to Richard. To stay here in the cabin alone without him was like death to her. It was difficult for him to leave her, the young brave figure who had stood beside him, gallantly, through their trials. He took both her hands and held them and looked down into her eyes. They were very full of sadness. He said:

'Little Anna, I shall come back.'

'I shall be here,' she said.

'I feel I ought to take you with me.'

'No. Much better not. Think how it would worry her, if she is ill, dying, Richard, and hears we are together. Tell her you have left me and gone to her alone.'

Richard bent and kissed her forehead.

'You're the bravest thing I've ever met, little Anna,' he said. 'I loathe leaving you. God bless you, darling. I leave you in Kiche's charge.'

'He'll look after me,' she said and smiled.

It was with the memory of her smile, a gallant thing, that Richard Strange drove away from Grey's cabin into the sunlit, sparkling wilderness toward Fort Yukon.

'Of course I shall go back to her,' he thought.

But Joanna, watching him out of sight till her straining eyes could only see man, sled and dogs as tiny blots on the horizon, suffered more poignantly than she had ever suffered. He had gone. She loved him so much that her heart was breaking in two. If Madge lived he must stay with her. He could not leave her. She might never see him again.

She wandered into the living room which had been their home for so many days. She saw his empty pipe on the table, his snow shoes. Suddenly she sat down by the table and began to cry. Tears poured down her face.

The voice of Kiche . . . urgent, anxious . . . penetrated her grief.

'Little mistress . . . quickly . . . we must bolt and bar the door and take our guns.'

She looked up quickly, her face distorted with pain.

'What is it, Kiche?' she asked dully.

'The white man whom you fear . . . Conrad Owen is coming over the snow,' said Kiche.

Joanna sprang to her feet. The tears dried on her lashes. Fear knocked at her heart. Conrad Owen had come back. Richard had gone.

The Indian said:

'Quickly, little mistress . . . in the cabin . . .'

'Don't let him get me, Kiche,' said Joanna, then turned back into the cabin, shut the door and barred and bolted it. Conrad Owen was the one man on earth of whom Joanna was afraid. He was a brutal, unprincipled creature. She knew that her fear of him was not without justification. Once he had taken her from Richard when Richard was dying. What might he not do now, when Richard was gone and she was unprotected except for the Indian?

She looked out of the window. Her heart beat rapidly. She took a rifle down from the wall — loaded it. She wondered if that horrible man, James Spence, was with him. But Conrad Owen was alone. She watched him drive up in his sled. The dogs strained and snarled under his cracking whip. He was clad from head to foot in furs. He looked a fine figure; blue eyes gleaming; face flushed; white teeth glistening between full red lips. Handsome in his florid, colourful fashion. Huge, every line of the big muscular figure suggestive of health and power and lusty spirits. But to Joanna he was repulsive, like a great animal.

She watched behind a window curtain and witnessed the meeting between Kiche and Conrad. Kiche stood like a bronzed statue . . . rifle in his hands . . . black eyes opaque, watchful. Conrad stepped off the sled and advanced toward him rubbing his cold hands together.

'Your mistress here?' he asked.

'No want to see Conrad Owen,' said Kiche.

Conrad stared, then burst into a roar of laughter.

'Don't want to see me, eh?' he guffawed. 'That's funny. Where is she, you — ' he swore at Kiche, then, all laughter vanished. 'In the hut, eh? All right. Get out of my way. I'm your master now and you do what I say.'

Kiche stepped in front of the door.

'Go further and Kiche will shoot,' he said quietly.

Conrad paused. For an instant he was baffled. He gave the Indian a look of murderous anger. His eyes wandered over the cabin. Then they narrowed to slits. He saw the top of a little boyish head through the living room window. Joanna's head. Joanna was in that cabin all right.

He smiled.

'I'll get her,' he said to himself. 'Holy smoke, does she think I'm afraid of her half-breed dog?'

Kiche's eyes were on him. Conrad dared not feel for the revolver in his hip pocket. But he tried a childish ruse and it succeeded. It invariably did, with more astute people than Kiche. He pointed to the cabin-window.

'Saints alive . . . look!' he cried excitedly.

Kiche, off his guard, turned his head. He was anxious in case some danger was threatening his beloved little mistress. He was lost. Immediately Conrad sprang at him. Kiche went down under the weight of that huge body. Conrad weighed fifteen stone. Kiche was like most men of his race; slight and lean and agile. But weight told in the fierce hand to hand fight that followed. Kiche fought, kicked, bit, wrestled gallantly on Joanna's behalf, but Conrad, through sheer strength and weight won the day.

The girl, watching through the window, felt her heart pump wildly. Every drop of blood drained from her cheeks. Conrad would win and then he would fight her. What chance had she against such a man?

She fingered her rifle. The palms of her hands were wet. She felt sick at the thought of shooting a man. But out here in the wild, frozen North, one must shoot to live. It was the survival of the fittest, the law of the Wild. No use being squeamish. She must either shoot Conrad Owen or he would take her.

By the time she got back to the window, Kiche was finished. Conrad had bound him with cord, hand and foot and relieved him of his knife. Kiche lay helpless on the ground, writhing, dismally conscious of his failure.

Conrad, panting, grinning victoriously, looked up to see a gun being levelled at him through the window. Joanna clear-eyed, cool, behind it.

'Move another step, Conrad Owen, and I'll put a bullet through you,' she said.

'Aw, come off it, kid,' said Conrad. 'Drop that gun.'

'Let Kiche go then.'

'I ain't going to do that.'

'Then I shall shoot,' said Joanna.

'Aw, hell that that,' said the trader. He looked anxiously, all the same, at the shining barrel of the gun. It infuriated him to be kept at bay by a slip of a girl. Why hadn't he thought that she might do something smart like this, he asked himself. He might have known John Grey's daughter wouldn't sit down and wring her hands. But he wasn't going to be defeated like this when he had won so far . . . got that half-breed under. He temporised.

'See here, Joanna, I don't mean no harm. Can't we be friendly? I used to be friends with your pa.'

'My father didn't know what you were like, Conrad,' said Joanna, keeping an eye upon him. Her heart was quaking. He was so very like a great animal standing there in all his furs, licking his red lips and screwing up his eyes in the bright sunshine.

'I only want to be friendly,' he said.

'Why have you come here? And why have you tied up my servant . . . if you are just friendly?'

'Aw, he tried to stop me coming to see you. That ain't being hospitable,' said Conrad in a wheedling voice. 'Surely you don't want to treat me like a stranger?'

'I treat you as an enemy which is what you are,' said Joanna. Her dark eyes never left his face. 'Go away and leave me alone.'

'But I come to look after you. You're all alone now the gentleman you favour has gone off,' he said.

'Mr. Strange is coming back at any moment,' Joanna tried to bluff him.

'Aw, hell to that,' said Conrad. 'His wife's sick back in the Fort. I just been there and heard all about it. Reckon you ought to be ashamed of yourself, carrying on with a married man . . . with a sick wife, too.'

Joanna's face went crimson. Her slim figure shook.

'How dare you? What do you know about it?'

'Everyone at Fort Yukon's talking . . . about John Grey's kid, living with the stranger and his wife sick and dying.'

'I don't believe it,' said Joanna, 'It's a

lie anyhow. We . . . we weren't living together. We shared this cabin. His wife knew. She left us here. Don't you speak to me like that . . . ' she broke off. Her hands shook so that she could scarcely level the rifle at the man who stood there, leering, jeering at her.

'Everyone said, seeing as how I was friendly with your pa, I ought to come and look after you, Joanna,' continued Conrad. 'The stranger's no good for you. He's a thorough wrong 'un.'

Joanna swallowed her rage. She refused to be baited by this man. Conrad may have heard that Richard's wife was ill at Fort Yukon, but that people were discussing her conduct she refused to believe. Folks minded their own business in the Yukon. The men hitting the gold trail up this part of the North had no time for gossip. It was just Conrad's low, nasty way of getting his own back at her. She wondered what to do, how to get him away. She couldn't stand here all day, pointing a gun at him. Her wrists ached now. How could she make him go?

'Why have you come?' She asked again, desperately.

'You know, Joanna,' he said. 'I'm mighty fond of you. I'm even keen to marry you. I'll give you more than that chap, Strange, can offer. Come along with me to Nome and get married, Joanna. Come on . . .'

She gave him a look of scorn.

'Thanks. I'd sooner die. What have you done with that other horrible man? I wonder you haven't brought him along to give you a helping hand again.'

The contempt in her voice maddened him. He ached to spring at her, seize her by the throat — shake the pride, the scorn out of her. He'd do it, too. If he had to stand out here in the snow all the afternoon and all the rest of the night. She'd get tired of keeping him covered; hungry, too. She was brave enough but she was only a slip of a girl. She wouldn't shoot him in cold blood.

Joanna was asking herself if she could shoot him in cold blood, and the answer was in the negative. If he made any attempt to rush at her, she'd shoot. But while he stood there, smiling, talking, how could she do it?

'Come on, drop the gun and let me in and be pals, kid,' he said in his wheedling voice.

'No,' she said. 'Never.'

'Never's a long time,' he said laughing.

Joanna thought:

'Richard . . . Richard . . . come back . . . Richard why didn't I go with you!'

Conrad Owen turned over in his mind the things he meant to do when he got inside that cabin . . . got to that girl. Damn her impudence, he thought, keeping him standing there on hot bricks, looking into the barrel of that damned gun.

He had not brought James Spence with him on this particular expedition because James Spence was no longer in the land of the living. He had expired after a severe attack of fever brought on by unaccustomed exposure to the fierce cold. He had weak lungs and he died in a week. But not before Conrad had made him hand over the papers concerning Joanna Grey, old Grey's heiress.

Conrad had the whole thing in his hands now. As soon as he could make Joanna his wife; bind her legally; he could produce those precious documents; prove to her that she was rich; then take her back to England to claim her money. But he was not going to let her know how rich she was — until she belonged to him.

The tussle between Joanna and Conrad went on for two solid hours. At the end of it Conrad was cursing. He was tired of standing there, cramped and chilled. But he would not give in. He jeered at her, invited her to shoot him several times. And several times Joanna tried to shoot . . . and failed. Her finger refused to pull the trigger. She had never murdered a human being in cold blood. She could not do it now. But she herself grew terribly tired and cold. The stove had gone out. The temperature was well below zero. The arm supporting her gun was rapidly growing numb. Her face was pinched and strained and she wondered how much longer she could hold out . . . if Conrad refused to go.

'Richard . . . Richard . . . ' she kept on repeating the name of her lover, as though it were a charm to drive away evil. But when she thought of him, driving to Fort Yukon to his wife, oblivious of her danger, her courage almost failed her.

The short day ended. Night came swiftly. Grey gloom veiled the white landscape. Dark shadows almost blotted out the figure of the man, swaying, like one drunk, with fatigue, but refusing to surrender.

The Eskimo dogs were hungry. They crouched in the snow and pointed their noses to the sky and howled.

'You still pointing that damn-fool gun at me?' Conrad asked the girl.

She gave a little groan.

'Go away . . . please, please go away.'

She could only just see him. He could only just see the faint outline of her in the window and the dangerous weapon that still covered him. The tussle went on. The atmosphere grew more and more tense. To the girl it was one long torture. To the man, an excitement now in spite of his hunger and fatigue. He would win in the end. He was sure of it . . . and then . . .

Suddenly he heard a low moan from the girl. His eyes flamed. He saw the slender figure sway, move. He ducked, and a bullet whizzed over his head through the gloom. Joanna had felt herself fainting and she had fired that shot in the last desperate effort to defend herself. Then Conrad straightened and laughed. He gave one bound toward the window and laughed again and again, stretching his great limbs. He had won. The poor little fool had fainted. The rifle had slipped from her hand.

He kicked the unfortunate Indian's prostrate body. Walked over it and opened the door of the cabin.

11

Joanna recovered from her fainting fit to find herself lying on the couch in the living room. She choked. Some whisky was being forced between her clenched teeth. She moaned, gasped and sat up. A long shudder passed through her body.

'Richard . . . ' she said.

She heard a laugh and saw Conrad Owen bending over her.

'Not Richard, my Beauty. But your sweetie whom you kept standing out in the rain . . . ain't that the newest song down South? Ha! Ha! Hee! Hee!'

His bellowing laughter seemed to fill the little room, to deafen Joanna's ears. His huge figure seemed to fill the room, too. Terror gripped her. She lay panting, white to the lips, staring at him. He had lit the lamp and pulled the curtains. He had taken off his cap and mittens and unbuttoned his coat, showing the coarse grey flannel shirt underneath. Outside the sled dogs were quiet. They had been given food. But a man moaned faintly. Kiche, the Indian, had been left out there, hand and foot bound in the snow. He would freeze to death.

Joanna cried out:

'Kiche . . . bring him in, let him have some food . . . you wretch . . . you brute . . . let him in!'

Conrad stuck his thumbs in his braces.

'Aw, quit that, kid. What's the fuss? Let the half-breed die, damn him. He would have killed me if he'd had half a chance.'

'He was trying to defend me. You can't blame him for that. Let him come in,' said Joanna.

Conrad stooped and picked her right up in his arms. He held her as though she had been a doll, her small feet dangling. He laughed delightedly when he saw a scarlet blush dye her face and delicate neck. Joanna Grey in her blue and white check apron, a little peach of a woman, he thought, and he'd never seen her like this before . . . all soft and feminine and frightened. It tickled his fancy. The Joanna he had known in the past had been like a boy. Tonight she was a woman . . . damn scared of him, too. Serve her right for keeping him out there so long.

'Let me down . . . put me down . . . ' Joanna said thickly.

He kissed her on the neck. She thought in agony what would Richard do if he could guess what was befalling her. She was alone in the cabin, locked in with this yellow-haired beast. Kiche was outside, dying in the bitter Northern night.

'Let me down. I ask it in my dead father's name,' she said, white and shuddering as he continued to cover her face with kisses. 'Conrad you were friendly with my father . . . oh, surely you won't . . . '

'How friendly were you with that

Englishman, huh?' he broke in, with his bellowing laugh again. His huge hands trembled about her. He was mad for her. That long battle out in the cold had not destroyed his desire. It had only added to the excitement. He looked down at the white little face, at the great velvet brown eyes, at the quivering flower of her mouth. 'How often did you lie in the arms of the Englishman, a married man, huh?' he added in a jeering whisper. 'Don't blush ... I know. I can bet what went on in these four walls when the wife's back was turned.'

'You beast,' said Joanna between her teeth. She writhed with humiliation, suspended there in Conrad's arms. 'You low beast ... to say such things. You lie ... you know you lie. Just because you've got a rotten, beastly mind ... you think Richard Strange is like you. He isn't. He isn't! He was good to me. He was decent. You don't know what decency is.'

Conrad only laughed. Her words

were feeble darts which failed to hurt him. His mind was too coarse to be wounded by a girl's contempt. He enjoyed baiting her. He didn't really care what had passed between Joanna and the Englishman. He intended to have her now. Her and her money.

He set her on her feet but kept an arm round her. He ran his fingers through her cropped hair, laughed every time she tried to duck him.

'Beauty,' he said. 'You needn't be so scared. You're going to marry me when we get to Nome.'

'I'm not,' said Joanna through her teeth. 'I'm not.'

'Aw, yes, you'll want to after tonight,' he said.

Her heart failed her. *After tonight.* Oh, God . . . God . . . how could she get away from him. She must.

He grew tired of teasing her and let her go. She stood there, swaying, sobbing under her breath with a hand against her bruised lips. Terror such as she had never known in any shape or form seized her now. To get away from Conrad Owen ... to get out of this cabin which was no more home and shelter but a place of menace where something terrible awaited her, was her one clear thought.

'After tonight you'll be pleased to marry me, Joanna,' she heard Conrad chuckle. 'Mrs. Owen the First, Ain't you proud?'

She looked from side to side like a trapped thing.

'Conrad, why are you tormenting me? Why do you want to force me to marry you if I don't want to?'

'Plenty of reasons, my girl,' he said. He seated himself at the table. 'Come now, fetch my supper. I could do with a bite. And a drink,' he added, drawing a flask from his hip pocket and uncorking it.

Joanna stared at him in horror. His yellow hair fell tangled over his red face. Yet he was sober. If he got drunk ... her knees sagged at the thought. She felt a film come over her eyes. She thought she was going to faint again. But she told herself that she must keep her head, do something drastic if she did not want to be at the mercy of this trader tonight.

'I'll cook your supper,' she said and turned and walked into the kitchenette. Once there alone, she lit a candle with a trembling little hand and stared blindly at a mirror over the basin. She began to sluice her face with ice-cold water — scrub her polluted lips. Her gaze was gradually caught and held by an iron. An old iron she used for her washing. She had always done her own laundry work out here in the Wilds. An iron was heavy and a useful weapon. If she threw it at Conrad's head it *might kill him*. Or it might only stun him. Even if it killed him she would have to risk that. She was up against a wall now fighting with her back to it. Either she must defend herself or surrender. And John Grey's daughter did not know the meaning of that word — surrender.

She was white as ivory when she

returned to the living room. Under the apron she carried something. Conrad gave her a curious glance.

'What you carrying, sweetie? A hot dish?'

'Yes,' she said, panting, and suddenly, with all her strength, threw the iron at his head. For her it was a tremendous effort . . . a supreme feat of accuracy and judgement. The man was unprepared for violent assault. He had sat still, staring. The iron struck his temples. She saw him reel and fall sideways out of the chair. He toppled on to the floor with a grunt. After that he neither moved nor spoke.

Joanna felt very sick. She forced herself to examine him. She shuddered when she saw the jagged cut on the left of the forehead where the iron had struck him. He was breathing. He was not dead. She gasped with relief. She could never have been happy again to know she had killed a human being even in self-defence. But how could she get away with Kiche — if poor Kiche were not already a corpse?

She could no longer remain in her old home. She must seek protection. And who could give it to her save Richard. She must go to Richard. She had nobody else in the world. She must see him, ask his advice. Her need was great.

She rushed into her bedroom. She sobbed as she put on her fur coat and leggings and found her cap and mittens. She gave one sick look at the unconscious Conrad, blew out the lamp and rushed from the cabin. The night was wonderful . . . clear . . . brilliant. The sky blazed with stars. A white, jewelled landscape, flooded by moon-light. Intense cold but no wind. An ideal night for a journey.

Joanna cut Kiche's bonds with a knife, and gave the Indian some of Conrad's whisky. The Indian was hardy and had life in him yet. His face soon broke into a grateful smile. He struggled on to his feet, rubbed his numbed hands. He was too great a stoic to show his agony to the white lady. Joanna said:

'Come, Kiche, quickly to Fort Yukon. Yes, the dogs have had food . . . they are fresh. Quickly. I have left Conrad Owen unconscious. I must get to Fort Yukon before he recovers.'

Ten minutes later Joanna was in the sled wrapped in furs. Her heart beat with a relief too great for words. Kiche drove the dogs. Snarling, straining, they ran quickly over the frozen waterway. And soon the cabin was left far behind them and Conrad Owen snoring in it. But Joanna, with tears pouring down her cheeks, tears of sheer relief after the strain of the last six hours, was going to her lover.

It was a long, cold drive. They stopped several times to rest the dogs, and each time Kiche lit a fire and Joanna warmed herself and ate a few biscuits and drunk the coffee he heated for her. But they never stopped for long.

It was grey dawn when they drew into Fort Yukon, a sleeping settlement, dreary and gloomy in the pallid Northern dawn which held none of the glamour or brilliance of the night.

Kiche stopped the sled at a loghouse, built on a fairly large scale, close to the massive Fort. It was a rough type of hostel.

Kiche knocked up the owner. A stout, grey-bearded man appeared at the door yawning and grumbling, with a fur coat over his pyjamas. He was less inclined to grumble, however, when he saw Joanna Grey. He had known and respected John Grey in the past.

'Why, surely it's Miss Joanna,' he said, stepping back to open the door wider. 'Come right in and welcome.'

Joanna walked into the warmth of the house, tears filling her eyes.

'Can I have a bed for the night, Matt?' she said. 'I can't pay you just now but — '

'Sure that's all right,' finished Matt. 'You're welcome. We've got a bed for you. Though I'm mighty full at present what with Mr. Strange and a doctor fellow from the States.'

The colour leapt to Joanna's cheeks. She drew off her mittens. Then Richard was here, in this very house. And she would see him. The sun was rising higher. It was daylight now. Richard would soon be awake and she would see him. Was it only yesterday that he had left her? It seemed to her an infinity of time had passed since their last meeting.

Richard Strange was already awake, up and dressed. He was going a journey and had prepared to catch a boat going Southland soon after seven. He came downstairs and saw Matt talking to a slim curly-headed girl in furs. And then his heart leaped to his throat.

'Anna!' He exclaimed.

She gave him one look, then walked into his outstretched arms.

'Richard,' she said. 'Richard — '

Matt gave the lovers one surprised look and shambled out of the room. A shabby dining room, dreary and untidy in the early morning light. But to

Joanna it had become heaven. Eyes shut, tears pelting down her face she lay against Richard's heart. He held her close, close, murmuring a hundred endearments. He caressed her hair, kissed her with warm kisses that brought all the life and colour back into her life.

'Darling, darling, beloved little Anna,' he said. 'What made you come? I'm glad — so terribly glad to see you. But why are you here? You must have travelled all night . . . you're cold, my poor little girl.'

'Not now I am in your arms,' she said.

He covered her face, her hands, with kisses.

'Oh, my dear, my dear little Anna.'

'I had to come,' she said. 'I was so frightened.'

'*You* — frightened? Of what?'

She told him the story of the frightful hours with Conrad Owen. His face grew grim as he listened. He held her more tightly. His heart beat hard against her own. He said:

'The swine . . . the foul swine . . . I could kill him . . . kill him for this. My poor little Anna.'

'Nothing matters now I'm with you again,' she said. But even as she said it her small hands clung convulsively to his arm. She added: 'I don't belong to you and I've no real claim on you, Richard, but where are you going? You're all dressed for travelling. Where are you going? Where is Mrs. Strange?'

'Madge is on her way to San Francisco,' he said. His face was troubled. 'The news we got of her was exaggerated. There was no question of her dying. When the doctor got her here he found her bad but not in immediate need of an operation. As she grew stronger he advised her to take the boat Southland and get to a big man in 'Frisco who could operate in a proper hospital and put her right. She seemed frightened of her condition of health and she went. She left a message for me here to say I must follow and be with her during the operation.'

'And you were going, of course,' said Joanna. Her arms fell away from him. 'Of course. You must go. It's your duty. You must go to her.'

And then she broke down, and cried like one whose dreams are shattered and whose hope is gone; cried desperately, her face hidden against his heart.

12

Richard held her tightly. He pressed the little dark head against his breast. Over it, his face was a mask of pain. He, too, could have cried. But he only stared blankly over her head at nothingness. He wished that he could say or do something to comfort her.

But what could he say or do? He was married to Madge and until that marriage was dissolved he had a duty toward her. She was ill. He must go to her. He loved this brave, adorable child in his arms more than he had ever believed it possible to love a woman. But he was not the man to be totally swept away on a blind, unreasoning tide of passion. Through all his aching desire to take her and hold her forever, the words 'honour' and 'duty' held him back from Joanna.

He shut his eyes and put his lips

against her hair.

'Little Anna, it's unbearable, my dear,' he said. 'Oh, Anna, my little love, don't cry like that. It breaks me up. I can't stand it. Anna don't cry . . . darling, darling, *please*!'

She heard the agony in his voice. She made an effort to control herself. For a moment she stroked his hair and his cheeks in silence. Then she whispered:

'Sorry, Richard . . . darling, darling Richard. I'm not being very brave.'

'Brave. You're always the bravest woman I have ever met,' he said hoarsely.

'Not over you. I love you so.'

'I love you. I don't want to leave you, I don't see how I can. You're alone, unprotected. It shows what might happen . . . that brute, Owen, getting at you like he did. How *can* I leave you?'

'How can you do anything else?' she said. 'You've got to go to your wife.'

'Well this time you must come with me.'

'If I do, what will happen when we

get to California?'

'I don't know,' said Richard grimly. 'But I do know I refuse to leave you up here in the Yukon to the mercy of the first beast that comes along.'

She shuddered and clung closer to him.

'If I come with you, Richard — I might get a job.'

'Yes, I suppose so. But when Madge's operation is over, she must be made to divorce me so that I can marry you. I've made up my mind to that.'

'Have you?' She was too tired, too utterly broken to argue with him now. There was a sharp, nagging pain in her head and she felt alternately hot and cold. She recognised the symptoms of fever. She drew away from Richard and put a hand over her eyes.

'I feel rottenly ill, Richard.'

'My dear, what is it?' he gave her an anxious, inquiring look.

'Fever, I think. I — I don't know whether I shall be able to go on with you, Richard.'

'Oh, Anna, you mustn't be ill now. We can't be parted again.'

'I don't know. Fate seems against anything else,' she said.

'The doc is still here — the American doc,' said Richard. 'He must see you, Anna, make you well again.'

'When does the boat go?'

'In an hour.'

'Do you think the doc can cure me in an hour?'

She sat down in a chair and leaned her aching head between her hands. All the thrill, the buoyant happiness of being with Richard again had gone. She was feeling really very ill; she, who so rarely had fever or went sick.

Richard began to worry. Little Anna would not give way unless she was bad. She was not that sort. He rushed out of the room to fetch the American doctor who had brought Madge to Fort Yukon.

The American came in, ten minutes later, looked at Joanna and took her temperature. He showed the thermometer to Richard.

'103,' he said. 'No wonder the little girl feels queer.'

'Oh, damn,' said Richard. 'Then she can't take this boat with me?'

'It would be plumb crazy,' said the doctor. 'Say, she oughter be in bed right now.'

Joanna, her heart sinking, looked at Richard. Her eyes were heavy and tragic.

'That's just — my luck, Richard.'

'It's damnable,' he said. 'I hate leaving you. I think I'll stay on here with you.'

'No, you can't do that. Madge is ill. I've only got a touch of fever. It will pass,' said Joanna, with a deep sigh. 'But Mrs. Strange is to be operated on. You must carry on.'

'If you'll come on to 'Frisco soon as you're fit, Anna.'

'I daresay that's what I'll do, Richard.'

'Very well, then I shall carry you up to bed now and make sure you're safe and sound, and leave you in Matt's care. He's a decent fellow.'

'Yes, please — carry me up,' she whispered.

The pain in her head was agonising now. She shut her eyes. She was shivering violently with fever when he lifted her and carried her up the wooden staircase to the little room he had just vacated. He laid her down on the bed and pulled the blankets over her.

'My poor little Anna. I'll get the doc to give me some dope for you. Will you be all right?'

'Yes. Only — just take me in your arms one moment, darling,' she whispered.

Richard lay down beside her. She turned her face to his shoulder and they both lay very still for a moment with their arms about each other. She felt weak and ill and the tears trickled down her cheeks. And the man, loathing the thought that he must leave her, tried to comfort her, feeling, himself, in the depths of depression.

'Don't cry, Anna, beloved.'

'It's silly of me . . . but I . . . I'm all in, Richard.'

'You're sick, sweetheart, and that business last night has shaken you up.'

'Yes.'

'Try to sleep . . . in my arms.'

'I can't. You're going soon. I keep thinking about that. Why have I got this rotten fever? Why can't I come with you? Richard, I'm losing my nerve . . . my courage.'

'You'll never lose it, little Anna. And look here . . . Murdock's Bank, Maine Street, 'Frisco will always find me. They'll know my address. You're to come out to me when you're well. Got any money?'

'Enough for my fare.'

'Very well. You'll come and I'll look after you.'

'How wonderful that will be,' she whispered.

'You little thing, how can I leave you with all these rough fellows about?' He said, anxiety returning to him. 'Don't go back to the cabin, Anna.'

'I'll have to go back. There's money locked up there. A despatch box of Dad's. Or I can send Kiche for it.'

'Don't go yourself, anyhow. I'm so scared now of anything happening to you.'

'I'll take care, Richard,' she whispered. 'And I'll pray, pray, Richard, that something will happen so that we can be together . . . one day.'

'Meanwhile you must take this,' he said. He pressed a roll of dollar-bills into her hand. 'No — don't refuse it. You must. I can't think of you without money, darling.'

She tried to smile as she took the roll from him. She bit hard at her lip to keep herself from crying again. And that was to be the end . . . for a long, long while, perhaps. When would they meet again?

The steamer going Southland left very early that morning. Ten minutes before the last siren hooted, Richard knelt beside Joanna's bed and held her passionately to his heart. He kissed her again and again. She, with all the stoic courage of her nature uppermost . . . tried to smile at him.

'Goodbye, goodbye, beloved little thing,' were his last words. 'Take care of yourself, for God's sake. Goodbye, sweetheart.'

'Goodbye, Richard, darling, darling lover,' she was hot, feverish, clinging with both hands about his neck. 'I'll come to you . . . you know that. Yes, you *must* go. I'll be all right. Oh, goodbye.'

And then Richard Strange tore himself away and left her.

Her pillow was soaked with tears, long after Richard had gone. Joanna was not brave once she had sent her lover to his wife. She lay in bed and cried until she was blind and sick with weeping. She was very sick and ill all that night.

For four or five days she was forced to stay in bed, and the fever racked her with pain. Physical illness almost obliterated mental agony. Matt and Kiche looked after her in their rough, kindly fashion, but she had to nurse herself most of the time. The doctor had left Fort Yukon and gone his way.

She struggled back to health; a thin little ghost of herself with eyes too big for her pinched face. She was astonished to find how weak and depressed she was. She had really suffered from an attack of influenza.

On her first day out of bed, she sat in Matt's dining room, by the fire and stared out at the vast white wastes of snow and spruce forest. It was all bleak and dark. The desolation seemed in keeping with her low spirits. The frozen Wild. The relentless snows against which men battled with puny strength and failed. Who could defeat the snows? Who could defeat the relentlessnesss of Fate . . . of what was yet to be?

When the short day ended and night came again, John Grey's daughter was more herself. But she was not quite the old Joanna. She was a woman who had learned the bitter pain of loving. Matt scratched his head and regarded Joanna in a puzzled way.

'Sure, you look rotten, Miss Joanna. Shouldn't you be going down South? The Yukon ain't no place for a lady.'

She smiled at him wanly.

'Don't you worry, Matt. I may be going South very soon. But I shall hate the city. I know nothing about the world beyond the Yukon.'

'That's so,' he said, pulling his grey beard. 'An' there's many a dark trap laid for a pretty girl in the cities. But ain't you English? Why surely, you could go to England.'

'One day I hope I shall,' she said.

'Ain't you got no relations?'

'Not that I know of,' she said wearily.

'Are you goin' to stay at the Fort a bit?'

'Till I'm stronger, yes,' she nodded.

Matt lit his clay pipe and walked to the window of the eating room wherein he had been talking to the girl.

'Hullo!' he said. 'Here's an old pal o' yours.'

'Of mine?' said Joanna. She walked to the same window and looked out. Then the colour left her face and her heart jumped.

A big man in furs was stepping off a sled, accompanied by another man in furs wearing a clerical collar. The first man was Conrad Owen. Conrad with a bandage round his head, looking sick and sorry for himself. The man with him, Joanna also recognised. 'Parson Pete', he was called. His reputation in the Yukon was not savoury. He had no right to his clerical collar. He had done deeds out here in the Yukon for which he should have been unfrocked, years ago. But that, Joanna did not know. He was not a prepossessing parson, anyhow. He was fat, and his bland smile made Joanna feel that something slimy and nasty lay behind it . . . behind the cloak of religion.

Her mind was concentrated upon Conrad at the moment. Would she

206

never get away from Conrad? She swung round to Matt, nervously.

'Matt . . . I'm scared . . . '

But the keeper of the hostel had gone to meet his new guests. Joanna was left alone. She was trembling. She asked herself what she could do . . . what Conrad would do next? Presumably Parson Pete had found him in the cabin, revived him and brought him here. Would Conrad tell everybody that she had given him that wound in the head? Would he leave her alone now? She must get away; send Kiche home for the money and take a passage on the next boat going to Nome.

13

Joanna and Conrad met for the first time in the eating room at supper time. When the fur-trader saw Joanna his eyes gleamed. A flush stained his face. Then he slouched toward her, hands in his trouser pockets.

'So here you are, my little wild-cat,' he said. 'This is where you've hidden yourself, hey?'

She did not answer, but turned her back on him. He grit his teeth; then laughed; a horrible, silky little laugh that made her shiver. He touched the nape of her neck where the dark curls clustered like a child's.

'You wait,' he said. 'You wait. I'll pay you back for what you did to me, my Beauty.'

She swung round on him, small fists clenched.

'You leave me alone, Conrad Owen.

Next time you try to bully me, I will kill you, I swear I will.'

'Ha! ha! Ho! ho!' He laughed. 'Kill me, eh? We'll see. And where's the Englishman? Left you again. Sick of you!'

She made a gesture of exasperation and walked away from him.

She locked herself in her bedroom that night. But in spite of turning the key she was nervous. She hated being under the same roof as Conrad Owen. And Parson Pete. She hated that clergyman. What lay in his mind? Several times during the evening she had caught his oily smile and it had seemed to her that he meant no good.

Matt, her only friend, to whom she confided some of her fears, had promised to protect her.

'Don't you worry, gel, about them men. I'll see no harm comes to John Grey's daughter,' he had said.

But Matt's weakness was drink and Conrad Owen saw to it that plenty of cheap and harmful spirit went down

Matt's throat that night.

By midnight Matt was roaring drunk. By one o'clock he was snoring and incapable. And then, when the hostel was in silence and darkness, Conrad carried out the plans he had made earlier in the evening.

He had no respect for locks and keys. He broke into Joanna's room without difficulty. The door was made of thin wood, easily shattered. Two mighty lunges of Conrad's great body and the crazy lock broke and a panel of the door splintered. Conrad was in Joanna's bedroom. She got up, roused from the uneasy sleep into which she had fallen. Dumb with terror, her great dark eyes stared at her enemy. Then she sprang up and opened her lips to shriek. But Conrad had her in his arms and pressed the palm of his hand against her mouth.

'No you don't. I've got you and you're coming with me for good this time, my Beauty,' he snarled. 'You've escaped me once too often. You're coming to be married, my gel, and then see if you can run away from your lawful husband.'

She writhed and moaned in his arms, but his strength was too much for a frail girl. Within two minutes she was helpless and gagged. He tied a scarf about her mouth; her hands and feet; and flung her over his shoulder as though she had been a doll. The blood rushed to her head . . . sick, dizzy, fainting, she hung there and wished she might have died before this could happen to her.

She knew very little of what happened beyond the fact that Conrad covered her in her own furs and carried her out to his sled where another man waited. Parson Pete. Still smiling, showing his broken, discoloured teeth. She was driven swiftly through the brilliant moonlit night over the sparkling snow . . . into the wilderness.

When she was unbound and the scarf and gag removed from her mouth she found herself back in her father's cabin.

Like a trapped creature, she swayed

in the centre of the room, looking from Conrad to the parson. She was still weak — unfit for this new disaster. Both the men seemed evil in the yellow light of the oil-lamp. The parson . . . with his hateful, leering smile. Conrad with the light of victory in his eyes. Joanna tried to face them calmly.

'What do you hope to gain by doing this sort of thing? Take me back to Fort Yukon at once, for God's sake.'

'No, my Beauty,' said Conrad. 'You've come to your wedding. The parson's here. I've had the certificate and the ring for weeks. Got 'em in Dawson City some time back before my pal, James Spence, died. You ain't going to get out of it now, Joanna. You're going to be married to me right now.'

She looked at him in horror.

'No, no, no — I'm not.'

'Yes, you are,' he said. He whipped out a revolver. 'See this?' he added, levelling it at her. 'You're for Kingdom Come, kid, if you say 'no'. This is your wedding and you're a willing bride

. . . else it's Death you'll marry tonight.'

'No, no, no!' her lips formed the words. 'Let me go! Let me go!'

Owen came up to her and took her hand.

'Come on, Pete. Say the words,' he said.

Parson Pete's smile never relaxed. He drew a shabby book from his pocket.

'I am ready,' he said in a high, nasal voice.

'I won't marry you — I won't!' Joanna panted. 'You can't force me. I'll die rather . . . *die* . . . '

Then she felt the cold muzzle of the automatic against her head.

'Would you sooner die, eh, kid? You'll be dead a hell of a long time. Aw, be sensible. Once we're married I'll take you straight to 'Frisco . . . to Noo York City . . . to London as well.'

Panting, beads of wet on her forehead, Joanna stared at the man. That cold thing against her forehead . . . it was horrible, to be so young, so full of ardent life . . . and to die. She thought of Richard whom she adored. She would never see him again; never again feel his arms about her or his lips upon hers. She couldn't bear that; couldn't bear to die. Yet if she lived . . . and was Conrad Owen's wife, wouldn't it be death in life? But supposing she consented — while there is life there is hope — and she might get away from him later.

'Conrad, listen,' she gasped. 'Take the revolver away.'

He smiled and put it back in his hip pocket.

'That's better, kid. Going to be a nice willin' bride?'

'Listen,' she said, and shuddered. 'If I . . . marry you, will you swear to leave me alone until I feel I can be a wife to you? Will you swear on this prayer-book?'

He scowled.

'Oh, I dunno 'bout that — '

'If you don't,' she broke in feverishly, 'if you won't, then I swear to you that I shall kill myself. I mean it. I'll do it somehow.'

Conrad looked at her uneasily. He knew Joanna's courage. She meant it. She might do herself in, he thought, and that wouldn't be what he wanted. Well, he could swear to leave her alone. Later he'd make her take his kisses. And after all it was her fortune he wanted as well as her kisses. He would get that, when they reached England.

'I'll swear that,' at length he said. 'You be my missus, kid, and I'll let you be, for a bit, anyhow.'

She was weak with fear and despair. In her ignorance, it never entered her head that this marriage would be illegal; that no man could force a woman at the point of a revolver, to marry him. Neither did she realise that Parson Pete was no longer a recognised member of the Church. Conrad knew, but Conrad did not mind. He only wanted Joanna to imagine herself legally tied up to him.

The unlawful ceremony was performed and the certificate signed. Joanna believed then that she was

Conrad's wife. Another frightful barrier between herself and Richard.

'What will Richard say?' she wondered. 'Not only *his* wife now, but my — husband.'

Her husband . . . this great, rough, yellow-haired brute. Like a nightmare that wedding . . . in the flickering light of the oil-lamp. Parson Pete making them man and wife . . . pronouncing sacred words he had no right to utter. Parson Pete was promised a handsome reward from Conrad for helping him force Joanna Grey into marriage.

The dreadful night passed. The unhappy girl who imagined herself to be legally Mrs. Conrad Owen now, locked herself in her old bedroom. Conrad and the parson were left to celebrate the occasion with much drink. Conrad was inflamed with triumph. He had got Joanna at last . . . and that promise he had made her would soon be broken. He didn't want the little fool to commit suicide. He'd leave her alone till she got accustomed to the idea of her marriage and then . . .

Face downward on her bed, Joanna lay motionless and dumb:

'Richard, I suppose I've lost you now altogether,' she thought.

She began to wonder why she had not let Conrad shoot her. She wondered when she could pluck up sufficient courage to shoot herself before he touched her. She was his wife now. Yes, she was sure of that. She knew nothing of the law. It seemed to her with the parson, the ring, the licence, it must be legal, even though she had been forced into it.

Yet life was sweet and she might see Richard again. She might. She clung to the hope . . . the only hope left . . . that if Conrad took her to 'Frisco . . . she might see Richard again.

14

Three weeks later Madge Strange lay in bed in an expensive nursing-home in San Francisco waiting for Richard to come and see her. He had been in 'Frisco for a fortnight now. He had seen her dutifully every day.

In Madge's hand was a newspaper. She read a paragraph with much interest. It stated that Miss Joanna Grey of the Yukon had married Mr. Conrad Owen of Dawson City and that the couple had left the Klondyke for 'Frisco. It gave Madge malicious pleasure to read that announcement. She had hated Joanna, the little chit, stealing Richard's affection. So she had married some man in the Yukon? How interesting. The paper was two days old and Richard had not mentioned that he had seen that announcement. Obviously he had not. Madge was certain he would have spoken about it because yesterday she had ironically asked him if he had heard from his 'friend' and he had flushed and said no . . .

Madge no longer had the slightest desire to patch up her differences with Richard. That feeling had only existed up North when Joanna had roused her jealousy. Madge was nearly well again after a small operation successfully performed. And Madge had grown more than ordinarily attached to the man who had operated on her. Boyd G. Harris, surgeon, of San Francisco. A big handsome American with plenty of money. And Boyd G. Harris had fallen quite madly in love with Madge. Her fair hair, her white skin, her good figure appealed to him. And her rather cold British superiority fascinated him. He had already told her that she must divorce Richard and marry him. Madge had made up her mind to do so. She was all the more keen to let Richard go free now that Joanna Grey was married to another man. How amusing it would be . . . one back on Richard for his treatment of her up in the Yukon.

When Richard visited his wife that afternoon he received news that was both a shock and a pleasure. Madge calmly informed him that she had decided to marry her doctor and remain in 'Frisco and that she would set Richard free as soon as he liked.

Richard, who had looked weary and depressed when he entered his wife's room, became a different being. His face was transformed. He stared at Madge incredulously. Was it true? Could it be true? He could go free . . . go to Anna and say 'I am free to marry you.'

He was overcome with emotion. But he took his wife's languid white hand and pressed it.

'My dear, if you and Harris will be happy . . . I'm glad. Because then we shall all be happy. You know how I feel — over Anna?'

She did not reply. But her eyes sparkled with malicious humour. The poor fool . . . when he got to the Yukon he would find his bird flown. Serve him right. And let him go and get his punishment. She wouldn't inform him of Joanna's marriage. He had not seen the announcement in the paper. He should find out for himself.

Richard left the nursing-home in a state of feverish excitement. He was going back to his hotel and from there he would wire to Joanna . . . wire the joyous news. Madge wanted to be free. They could be divorced. And soon, soon he would be able to have and hold Anna forever . . . his wonderful, brave, beautiful little Anna.

The great city, teeming with traffic and people, golden with the warm Californian sunshine, seemed like heaven to Richard today.

He rushed up to the reception-bureau at the big hotel, facing the fine harbour, where he had stayed since he arrived in 'Frisco. He wanted to send that wire to Joanna at once. Poor little Anna whom he imagined was still at

Fort Yukon with Matt.

Then his heart gave a violent jerk of astonishment and delight. He saw a girl standing by the bureau; a small slim figure in a dark blue silk dress; a big blue hat on her curly head. A girl with a pale, wistful face and huge brown eyes staring mournfully under their long lashes.

He gave her one rapt look, then rushed to her.

'Anna! Little Anna! You've come! You're here!' he cried.

She started and stared at him. The colour flooded her face. She instinctively moved toward him:

'Richard . . .'

He gripped her hands. His whole body tingled with delight at at the unexpected vision of her. Anna, as he had never seen her before. Not the fur-clad boy-girl of the frozen North. But a little lady in her blue silk dress; slim legs in gossamer stockings; small feet in black patent shoes. A changed, exquisite Anna. And he adored her

. . . adored her from the crown of the darling curly head to those small, slender feet.

'Anna, when did you get here? I was just going to wire to you. I thought you were thousands of miles up North. Sweetheart, are you well again? You look thin and pale. But are you all right? Had you written to my bank?'

She could not speak. She could do nothing but stare up at him. She was dumb with the pain of her thoughts; the memory of the big yellow-haired man who was her husband, Conrad, who had just gone into the bar for a drink. He always went straight to the bar wherever they were. She shivered at the memory of their journey from Fort Yukon. He had kept his promise so far and left her alone. But it was frightful to be with him . . . all day.

'Anna,' said Richard again. 'Do you know what I was wiring you, darling? I'm free. Madge wants her freedom. When the divorce is through, I can marry you. Oh, my dear, my dear, say you're glad . . . '

He paused breathlessly, staring down at her. Then his smile faded. For he saw a queer look in her eyes.

'Anna,' he said. 'Anna, what is it?'

She held up her left hand. He saw a broad gold wedding-ring on her finger. He stared at it speechlessly. She said in a small unhappy voice:

'It's too late, Richard. Too late. I was married to Conrad Owen up in the Yukon . . . three weeks ago.'

He looked down at Joanna as though he had not heard correctly. He said, very slowly:

'You were *married* to Conrad Owen. *Married*?'

'Yes,' she said. She shuddered violently all through her small slim body and turned from his amazed eyes as though she could not bear to look into them. 'Yes,' she repeated. 'It's rotten isn't it, Richard, that you should come and tell me you can get your freedom . . . now!'

Then Richard woke up. The blood

surged to his temples. He gave a swift look round the vestibule of the hotel in which they were standing and took Anna's arm.

'We can't talk here,' he said. 'And I am going to have this out with you, Anna. It's absolutely shattered me. My dear, it can't be true. I can hardly think straight.'

She nodded her head. She moved acquiescently with him as he guided her through the vestibule into a smoking-room which was deserted. He shut the door, then drew her on to a sofa.

He held both her hands in a grip that hurt her. He stared at her as though trying to understand. He could not believe that Anna was married . . . and married to Conrad Owen of all men in the world.

'My dear,' he said hoarsely, 'Speak to me. Tell me everything. Anna, Anna, why in God's name have you married Owen?'

She took off her hat with a weary gesture. His heart was wrung by the sight of her face. It was pinched and pale. She looked up at him with suffering eyes.

'Of course I didn't do it of my own free will. He made me marry him. And we haven't lived together. I never will belong to him. I love you. I will never love any other man on earth.'

He gave a cry and put an arm about her. She did not resist him and the next moment her own arms were about his neck. She told him the whole story. He held the shuddering little figure and listened. His face grew dark with anger. That such a thing could have happened. To Anna — his little love — that frightful wedding in John Grey's cabin. It was outrageous. But of course it was not legal. His poor terrified little Anna.

'Hush, sweetheart — hush — don't cry,' he said. 'Listen Anna. It's all right. I understand. You were forced into it. Anna, you're going to be free. You needn't worry. That swine can't hold you. A marriage by force is not legal.'

She raised her head from his shoulder and looked at him eagerly:

'Oh Richard, are you sure?'

'Certain. It was a devil's act. Tell me, has he hurt you? Has he dared to touch you?'

'No . . . he hasn't even kissed me. I haven't let him. It was a bargain . . . that if I married him he would leave me alone for the time being, anyhow. I said I would kill myself if he wouldn't agree.'

Richard held her closer.

'Anna . . . don't think of such a thing. I know I ought not to have left you at Fort Yukon.'

'You had to. Your wife . . . but now . . . ' Joanna's voice broke. 'Now you say she will set you free?'

'Yes. She doesn't want me any more. She has found someone else. A doctor . . . the chap who operated on her, Anna. Just sheer luck. I'd never have dreamed Madge would do it. But it's just what we needed . . . each of us to find someone else . . . the right one. We can get a divorce now — at once.'

'Only a few weeks ago that would have opened the gates of paradise to us,' said Joanna in a tragic voice. 'Now there's this marriage of mine.'

Richard took her hand and pulled off that gold band.

'You're not married to him, Anna.'

'But how can I prove that I was forced into the marriage? How can I prove it? That dreadful parson . . . he will swear I married Conrad willingly.'

Richard gnawed his lips. He still held Joanna close to him.

'Anna, we'll go to a lawyer,' he said. 'We must have legal advice. I know there will be a way out. Parson Pete, as you call him, can't have such a fine reputation in the Yukon if he is that sort of fellow . . . his word wouldn't hold good. Probably he hasn't even the right to perform a wedding.'

'But we had the licence and ring . . . Conrad bought them in Dawson City,' said Joanna.

Richard nodded grimly.

'Maybe. But the marriage is illegal.

And why is that fellow so mad to marry you at all costs?' He added. 'If it was just because he wanted you — and lord knows you're beautiful and sweet enough to make a man crazy for you — he wouldn't have left you alone all this time, wouldn't consider your wishes for one instant. He must have an ulterior motive. I'm sure of it, Anna. Otherwise he'd have forced you into his arms and not cared whether you killed yourself afterwards or not. He isn't the type to wait patiently for a woman . . . unless he has something big at the back of his mind.'

'I can't think what it is, then,' said Joanna helplessly. 'What motive can he have for marrying me?'

'I'm trying to think,' he said.

The door was pushed open. A big yellow-haired man came in.

'You seem to forget you're Mrs. Conrad Owen, Joanna,' he said in a snarling voice.

Joanna drew away from her lover. Richard sprang to his feet. And the next moment, before she knew what had happened, Richard had sprung at Conrad Owen and hit him, savagely, across the mouth.

15

Joanna gave a startled cry.

'Richard — take care . . . Conrad . . . don't . . . '

Her voice died away and she stumbled to the door and stood with her back to it. Richard Strange and his enemy were fighting . . . fighting like two madmen . . . with clenched fists and bared teeth and muscles taut. For weeks Richard had wanted this battle. Ever since Owen had taken Anna away; left him for dead in the lonely, snow-bound cabin, he had wanted to get at Owen. To make him pay for what he had done to Anna . . . make him suffer for Anna's suffering.

Conrad yelled at him . . . eyes bloodshot . . . face scarlet with fury.

'Think you'll get the better of me, do you? I'll knock you to a jelly, Mr. Englishman!'

'This for all you've done to Joanna . . . for your blackguardly tricks . . . ' Richard panted and struck out at the menacing, crimson face of his enemy. 'This for forcing an innocent child into that damned farce of a marriage.'

'Farce, eh? Hell to that!' shouted Conrad and struck back wildly.

Conrad Owen was a huge man of great physical strength. Richard was slim; boyish; a head shorter. But Richard had learned to box in his youth. And sheer brute strength has little chance against scientific boxing. Richard was as lean, as fit, now, as he had ever been. He had recovered completely from his illness up in the Yukon which had only been brought about by semi-starvation.

Today he was brimming with life . . . with power. He tingled from head to foot with it. He was fighting for Anna. He wouldn't be knocked to a jelly by this great, hulking ox of a fellow.

Richard laughed as he fought. And the girl, leaning against the wall

. . . watched him and thrilled. She could glory in such a lover. She was afraid for him but all the primitive woman in her exalted in this fight. A fight for her. She was used to such scenes up in the frozen North. But never had two men fought for her before. She watched, her heart shaking, her eyes brilliant with excitement.

Then Conrad Owen went down . . . down like a felled ox . . . bleeding from the nose and mouth, lips cut by Richard's clenched fists. A smart blow to the right of his jaw had finished Conrad. He was down and out. The smoking room of the hotel spun round him.

Richard calmly put on his coat again.

'Now, my friend, you will give me an explanation of this marriage,' he said grimly.

Conrad was inarticulate with rage. Joanna turned from the sight of the bruised, bleeding face and shuddered. He staggered on to his feet; sat down on the sofa, and put his head between his hands while he wiped the blood from lips and nose. Then he spoke to Richard, voice thick, husky with rage:

'I'll get you for this, Richard Strange . . . blast your eyes. I'll get you for it . . .'

'You're too fond of threats, you great bully,' said Richard. 'Let's have straight talking. Anna — '

'Joanna's my wife,' broke in Conrad. 'Remember that, damn you!'

'She's not your wife at all,' said Richard. 'You can't put a revolver at a girl's head and make her marry you.'

'Who said I did?' Conrad's bruised face shot up and he looked malevolently from Richard to Joanna. 'Who can prove she didn't marry me willingly, huh? I've got her licence . . . she signed her name right enough and Parson Pete will back me up.'

'I shall see a lawyer about that,' said Richard.

'Aw, go to hell,' said Conrad furiously. 'You can't alter no facts like that, with all your blasted lawyers.

Joanna's my wife.'

Richard narrowed his gaze.

'Why do you want her so badly, eh, Owen?'

'Why do *you* want her?' Owen laughed coarsely.

'Answer my question. What's behind this mad desire of yours to have her at all costs?'

Conrad lowered his gaze. He shrugged his shoulders. His bleeding lips widened in a sudden grin. The papers which James Spence had given him were safe in his pocket. He wasn't going to let Richard Strange know about them. Nor Joanna either. In good time, when he'd got Joanna safely to England, he'd tell her about her grandfather's will. Meanwhile he wanted to be rid of the interfering Englishman. He looked up again . . . a sly look from the girl to Richard.

'When you've proved our marriage wasn't legal you can come back,' he said softly. 'But just now, you can get

'. . . see? We're Mr. and Mrs. Conrad Owen and we'll remain so.'

'Anna shall not stay with you,' said Richard.

'What, going to run off with a married man? Shocking!' sneered Conrad Owen.

Joanna's pale little face flushed scarlet.

'My wife and I are getting a divorce,' said Richard. 'When it's through I am going to marry Joanna.'

'Not if I know it,' said Conrad.

'Richard,' said Joanna. 'I can't stand any more of this. I shall pack a bag and move to another hotel at once.'

'I think that's a very wise move, Anna,' he said.

'To hell with that — ' Conrad started to shout.

'Please be quiet,' broke in Joanna, turning to him. 'I've had three weeks of you, Conrad, and it's enough. I was stupid enough to believe our marriage was legal. Richard says it isn't so I shall not stay another moment with you.'

'He's got to prove it isn't legal, first,' said Conrad.

'Very well. He intends to. At the moment he is still tied, and I'm not sure whether I am or not, so I shall stay in a hotel by myself. And if you follow or molest me — '

'I'll set the police on him, Anna,' said Richard shortly. 'Don't you worry.'

Conrad smiled.

'I'll follow and neither you, Mr. Englishman, nor the blasted police'll prevent me.'

Joanna gave Richard a despairing look.

'I daresay he means it, Richard. And if he's simply going to follow me to the next hotel, I might as well stay here.'

'All right,' said Richard. 'Then I shall know what to do. I happen to be staying in this hotel, myself. I'll look after you, that's all.'

'He won't hurt me, as a matter of fact,' said Joanna calmly. 'He knows that if he lays a hand on me, I shall throw myself out of the window. He knows that.'

Richard hesitated.

'Anna, if only I could take you right away — '

'You can't, dear Richard, till you're free yourself. There are so many tangles.'

'I certainly don't want you brought into my divorce,' he said gloomily. 'Oh, my dear — are you sure you'll be all right? Look here — I've got a business appointment. I must keep it. Then I'll come along back to you. And I'll look up a lawyer who's a pal of mine. He'll advise us. You are sure you will be all right, Anna?'

'Sure,' she said. 'Conrad and I have separate rooms. He won't worry me.'

Conrad watched darkly. But he said nothing. Richard Strange had beaten him today and he had had enough punishment. He didn't want to fight Richard again. But when he was alone with Joanna, he'd show her who was master . . . he'd show her! He knew exactly what he meant to do next.

'Remember,' said Richard. 'If you need me, my room is No. 490.'

'And if you have anything to tell me, after you have consulted a lawyer, Richard . . . my room is 241.'

'He won't need you, my gel, he'll need an undertaker if he comes round after you again,' Conrad muttered viciously. But Joanna did not hear him. She looked at Richard. He took her hand and pressed it.

'It'll be all right, Anna. Leave things to me. I'll have good news for you soon. And meanwhile take care . . . '

Richard walked out of the hotel into the hot sunshine . . . He walked down the broad sidewalk to his appointment and could think of nothing but Joanna.

Joanna left alone with Conrad, faced difficulties which she had not antici-pated when she had told her lover that she would be all right. She was not afraid for herself. Even death had few fears for Joanna, providing that she could not share life with her lover. But Conrad was cunning. He did not threaten her. Did not lay a finger on her, much as he wanted to. He ached to take her and break her spirit, make her crawl to him. But this he dared not do. He did what he dared. He sat opposite her in the smoking room where Richard had left them and it was Richard he used as a lever to separate her from him.

'Now you listen to me, Joanna Owen,' he said. 'You're my wife. And I'm telling you this. If you don't pack up and come along with me, this minute, and let the Englishman go his own way, I'm going to put a bullet *straight through his head.*'

Joanna eyed him steadily. But she was frightened.

'You wouldn't dare.'

'Oh yes, I would, and I will,' said Conrad. He stood up and whipped a revolver from his coat-pocket. It flashed in the sunlight. 'See this? It can kill a man easy. I'm not the fellow to be threatened and treated like pulp. I'm not the chap to take a licking kindly. Your Mr. Strange knocked me out, today. But by gum, I'll blow his brains out next time he comes back into this hotel. So you'd better make up your mind to leave it with me — quick.'

She put her hands behind her back. They were cold with fear for Richard now.

'You wouldn't dare ... you'd be electrocuted. You don't mean it. You're trying to scare me.'

'Am I?' He came close to her, his eyes glittering. 'Mark me, Joanna, I'm not. *I mean it*. I'll sit in the electric chair, or go to gaol, anything you like, but first I'm going to get Mr. Richard Strange. Unless you come away with me right now.'

She looked round as though seeking for help, for advice. And there was nobody to give it. She knew Conrad was making no idle threat. He was half mad with rage. He was the type to shoot ... and shoot to kill. He had been born and bred in lawless country where men shot each other down and got away. He had no respect for human life. She pictured Richard coming back to the hotel. Richard shot down, dying, dead. It was more than she could bear.

'No,' she said under her breath. 'You can't shoot him — you can't!'

'I can and will,' said Conrad. He came right up to her now and thrust his face to hers. 'I swear on my oath, unless you come away with me now, I'll murder that chap!' he said.

She looked at him wildly.

'No, no.'

'Yes. Choose, Joanna. Will you come with me or will you see him shot?'

'Where do you want me to go?' she panted.

'New York . . . then England.'

'Oh my God . . . ' she drew a hand across her eyes. To put thousands of miles between her lover and herself again. It was unthinkable. But equally unthinkable that Conrad should keep his oath and end life for Richard.

Richard who loved life.

She thought, frenziedly:

'I'd better humour Conrad now. I must. I daren't risk it. But I won't go away with him. I'll go away alone. Anything . . . rather than spend the rest of my days with Conrad Owen.'

She matched her brains against his cunning.

'Listen — don't shoot him — I'll come with you.'

'Ah!' Conrad laughed and pocketed his automatic. 'Right now, then.'

'Yes, now,' she said.

'I'll call an automobile,' he said. 'Our bags ain't unpacked. Come on. Put on your hat.'

Joanna was silent a moment. Then she said:

'Wait, Conrad. I left my coat up in my room. Fetch it for me.'

'You'll wait here.'

'Yes.'

'Any hanky panky and I'll put a bullet throught that fellow's head,' began Conrad.

'Oh, go and fetch my coat,' she said. 'I'll be here.'

He eyed her narrowly.

'A page can fetch it. Come on. I ain't going to lose sight of you.'

Desperately she said:

'Oh, all right.'

He gave her no chance to escape. She felt very sick when she found herself in a car with him, being driven to the station. The sun was setting. She wondered what she could do next. How she could get away from him. But at least she had saved Richard. There would be no bullet waiting for him when he returned to his hotel.

How could she let him know what had happened? She felt she would go mad if Conrad forced her out of San Francisco without giving her any opportunity to communicate with her lover.

At the big station she made a last, desperate effort to hoodwink Conrad. She said calmly enough:

'I'm really sick of all this. I feel now

I'd like to get to New York and start another life.'

Conrad stared.

'You mean that? Aw, that's grand, Joanna.'

'Yes, I'm tired of all this bickering,' she went on. 'Conrad, go and see to the seats in the train . . . and I'll get the tickets. How much money shall I need?'

'I'll give it to you. Aw, honey, if you're going to be nice to me, I'll sure give you the earth,' he cried.

He was a very silly man for all his cunning and scheming. He was also very conceited. He took it for granted that Joanna would settle down to the thought of life with him in time. He had no suspicions when he gave her a thick roll of dollar-bills and left her to get their tickets.

Joanna's forehead was wet with nervous strain. Her heart galloped wildly. She hurried not to the booking-office, but to a call box. She put a call through to the hotel. She was shivering with nerves when she asked if Mr.

Strange had come in yet.

Her relief was enormous when the reception clerk told her that Mr. Strange had come in a few minutes ago and that they would connect her with his room. A second later she was talking to him and the world which had been gloomy and unhappy was suddenly flooded with light.

'Anna, Anna, why have you gone away?' he asked. 'When I asked for you and they said Mr. and Mrs. Owen had left with their luggage I nearly went mad.'

'I had to go. I'll explain,' she panted.

And she told him of Conrad's threat . . . and how she had given him the slip, and come to the call-box. 'What shall I do now, Richard?' she asked.

'Wait for me. I'll come to you,' said Richard's urgent voice. 'Dearest, look here, we'll go away together. Yes, I don't care. We can't go on like this. Listen. I've seen a lawyer. He says your marriage to Owen can be proved illegal. You're free, darling, free, and Madge is going to set me free. It's madness for us to separate now. You need me to protect you. I must — I will come with you.'

She trembled from head to foot.

'Oh, Richard, where shall we go? Back to the Yukon?'

'Anywhere you like,' he said. 'I shall never know an instant's peace while you're alone.'

'Whatever you do, you mustn't risk staying at the hotel,' she said nervously. 'When Conrad discovers I've got away, he'll be like an enraged bull. He'll rush back to the hotel and try to get you. Richard, darling . . . you must leave at once. For God's sake, don't lose time.'

Her excitement made him catch fire. He gave a brief laugh. He felt mad, ready to do any mad thing, risk anything. But he would not be separated from Anna any longer. Not even the conventionality, the regulations of man-made laws should divide them. They would go away together.

'Wait for me,' he said in a voice that

thrilled her through and through. 'Where can you hide yourself from Owen? In the Ladies' Waiting Room. Yes. Wait there. It'll take me a few minutes to throw my things into my grip and get to the station. But watch out for me.'

'Yes,' she said breathlessly. 'I won't let Conrad see me. Only for heaven's sake, be careful . . . get away from the hotel quickly.'

'All right. Oh, Anna, I adore you . . . I adore you so!' he said.

'I love you.'

They had suffered enough . . . been parted long enough. He was going to take her away and when his marriage was dissolved nothing on earth should part them again.

In the Southland Hotel, Richard Strange, smitten with the same divine madness, packed a bag and prepared to depart. Ten minutes after he had spoken to Joanna he was on the front-steps of the hotel, waiting for the commissionaire to fetch a car. And then, from the opposite side of the road, another car wheeled and stopped at the kerb before the hotel and a big yellow-haired man sprang out. A man with murder in his heart and in his gleaming eyes. He gave one look at Richard. Richard looked at him. The next moment there was a report. Richard Strange flung up his arms and toppled down the steps and lay there in the twilight on the sidewalk, horribly still.

16

In the Ladies' Waiting Room at the station, Joanna waited for Richard to come back. She waited for what seemed to her an interminable time. She sat down. She walked about. She sat down again; nervously biting her under-lip; trying not to worry, but feeling frightfully worried.

Richard had had more than enough time to get to the hotel and back. He could have done it twice over. Either something had detained him; or he had met with an accident; or he had changed his mind and decided not to fling up the whole of his career and go away with her. So many possibilities. Joanna considered them all. The wild fever of delight which had come upon her at first when Richard had made his decision to elope with her had gone. She had a queer cold feeling, almost a presentiment of evil.

She longed to go out to a station call-box and ring up the Southland Hotel; see if Richard had returned. But she dared not go out into the open station. Conrad might be there; still looking for her.

Two hours went by. At the end of that time Joanna felt sick with worry. She decided definitely that he must have met with an accident; or even that he had come up against Conrad; a Conrad mad with jealousy and hatred. Very white, and cold, Joanna emerged from her hiding place. She felt that she must telephone through to the hotel . . . or go mad.

Carrying her suitcase she walked with determination into the open. She became one of a hurrying throng of people catching trains or emerging from them. Trains shrilled . . . porters shouted . . . the usual din of a big, busy terminus deafened Joanna. She shrank from it all. She had not yet grown used to the city . . . to the noise and clamour of it.

It was pandemonium to her who from babyhood had lived in the strange and wonderful silence of the vast frozen Wild.

Joanna walked to one of the call-boxes from which she had telephoned two hours ago.

'Richard . . . Richard,' she thought, 'where are you? What has happened? . . .'

And then her heart seemed to leap to her throat and choke her. Her whole body-tingled. She saw Conrad Owen striding toward her through an archway. A strange-looking Conrad with wild eyes. Her tongue clave to the roof of her mouth. Her knees trembled. Conrad. What misfortune, to run straight into him like this as soon as she came out of the Waiting Room. Just what she had dreaded and she had not even had time to ring through to the hotel.

Conrad saw her and reached her side. He took her arm with fingers that gripped like steel-bands. He snarled at her.

'So here you are . . . you little hell-cat . . . running away from your husband.

But you won't run away again, my Beauty. That you won't. Come along. We're for the next train, out of this by town!'

She tried to release herself . . . panting . . . shivering.

'No, I'm not going with you. I'm not. Let me go.'

'You are coming with me, Joanna. Right now.'

'No, no!' she said.

He looked furtively over his shoulder. Licked his lips. He seemed to her strange and wild and terrible. Yes, there was a terrible look in those glittering blue eyes. A look that made her quail. She added, in a whisper:

'Conrad, what have you done? What have you been doing?'

He laughed down at her then. It was a snarl rather than a laugh, showing his white teeth like one animal that menaces another.

'I've shot your lover, Joanna . . . shot him like I said I would. That's what I've been doing.'

Silence. Joanna stood rigid. She stared up at him. Her eyes were enormous. The noisy station . . . the world itself seemed to whirl and revolve about her. But she did not faint. She was conscious only of the most hideous sensation of grief. And now she understood all her fears . . . her presentiments . . . This was the end of her waiting for Richard. This was the end of *everything*. With unnatural calm she spoke to Conrad.

'You've — shot — Richard?'

'Yes . . . I warned you I would . . . if you tried any tricks.'

'Is he — dead?'

'Yes,' said Conrad. 'Dead as a doornail.'

She shuddered from head to foot. Her eyelids closed. Richard . . . dead . . . dead as a doornail. Conrad had shot him. It was true — he had warned her. Therefore she was responsible for Richard's death. If she had not telephoned to him. If she had not asked him to come . . . let him come . . . this would not have happened. If she had not run away from her husband, it would not have happened. Conrad had kept his frightful vow . . . and he had shot Richard . . . dead.

'It's your own fault,' Conrad's voice reached her as from a distance. 'You ran away from me. I told you I wouldn't put up with that hanky-panky. You 'phoned him, didn't you? I know. I saw him come out of the hotel with his luggage. Meant to join you, didn't he? But I got him first. Ha! ha! ha!'

The laughter seemed to her maniacal. She opened her eyes and looked at him. She wondered if he was out of his mind. Yet it was nothing to Conrad Owen to shoot a man. In the Yukon he had shot men, before. But here in San Francisco it seemed worse. He ought to be arrested. They electrocuted men in America, didn't they, for murder? He was a murderer . . . *Richard's murderer*.

Joanna suddenly screamed and tried to wrench her arm away.

'Let me go . . . let me go, you vile creature . . . you murderer . . . let me go . . .'

'Shut up, you little fool. D'you want folk to hear?' he said.

He was as white as she was now. For this certainly was 'Frisco where men could be arrested and thrown into gaol for shooting . . . and Conrad had no wish to be put into gaol.

It was not that he was afraid of being tried for murder. He did not think that Richard Strange was dead. But he had told Joanna that he was dead. To put all this love-rot out of her mind. He wasn't going to lose her or her money now he'd got so far.

After he had shot Richard . . . seen him go down like a ninepin, Conrad had vanished in the thick of the crowd before anybody had had time to detain him. By this time of course there would be a hue and a cry. He must get away — out of 'Frisco . . . quickly.

Richard had been unconscious. Conrad took it for granted that he would be taken by an ambulance to hospital and that when he recovered his senses (if he were not fatally hit) he would give the name of his assassin. Conrad decided that he would take Joanna to New York quickly and thence to England where he would change his name and marry her all over again, legally this time.

'Come on, Joanna,' he said. 'Richard Strange is done in. No use hanging round after his corpse. Come on with me.'

'Oh, no — not I.' Joanna drew away from him.

The numbed feeling had left her. She was beginning to feel acutely. She was wild with pain. Her darling, darling Richard dead . . . killed by this monster. This monster of iniquity who had been the cause of half their suffering, who had tormented her and bullied her for months on end. Nothing would induce her to go with him now.

She was Richard's brave Anna, self-reliant, fiercely independent. If Richard were dead she would face life alone all the rest of her days.

She lifted a small face that blazed with hatred at the man.

'Let me go,' she said between her teeth. 'If you keep me — if you try to bully me, I'll tell the first policeman I see what you've done.'

'Aw, come off it,' muttered Conrad. 'You can't blame me. You drove me wild with jealousy. I'm mad about you, Joanna, and — '

'Don't dare say another word,' she broke in. 'If you want to sleep in a prison-cell tonight . . . you can do so. I am warning you, now, Conrad Owen.'

He flushed darkly.

'Aw, listen — ain't I your husband?'

'No. Richard had seen a lawyer and he says our marriage was illegal. You've no claim on me at all. And I hope I shall never never see you again . . . you vile monster . . . '

The sweat stood out on Conrad's forehead. He moistened his dry lips with the tip of his tongue.

'Joanna — listen — aw — you can't

desert me now. Listen — I got something to tell you. Something you don't know. I got news for you — about some money you own — Joanna.'

He stopped. He was baffled; defeated at his game by this slip of a girl whose courage was and always had been unfailing.

She turned and ran from him. He ran after her, shouting her name:

'Joanna — aw, Joanna — stop!'

She looked back over her shoulder . . . her eyes dark and furious.

'Haven't you done enough . . . you've killed Richard,' she panted. 'Now, if you follow me, you go to prison. I swear it!'

He fell back — craven coward — afraid. He knew that Joanna would keep her word. He had lost her through his own passionate, brutal folly. Fool that he was. He stood there alone, cursing himself.

Joanna sprang into the first car for hire which came her way.

'Southland Hotel,' she said.

17

Darkness had fallen over San Francisco when Joanna reached the Southland Hotel. She was like a figure of stone when she emerged from the taxi. She was quite composed, mistress of herself and the situation. She had left Conrad; finished with him.

'My Richard . . . oh, my lover,' she whispered as she walked into the hotel. 'You can't be dead. You can't be. Oh, my Richard, my darling one . . . '

She walked up to the reception-bureau.

'Can you tell me — anything about — Mr. Strange?' she asked the clerk.

The girl shoved a pencil behind her ear and ceased chewing gum for a moment.

'Mr. Strange? Why sure. He was shot outside the hotel this evening.'

Joanna gripped the edge of the

bureau. Two red spots burned on her cheeks.

'Was he — killed?'

'They say he was dying when he was taken away to hospital.'

Joanna did not, could not speak. The reception-clerk stared at her curiously. Something in the girl's great dark eyes disturbed her. She told a friend, later, that she had never seen such naked pain in the eyes of any human being before. She was a kind-hearted woman and she spoke kindly, now:

'Say, are you sick? Aren't you Mrs. Conrad Owen? You booked rooms here, then left suddenly, didn't you?'

'Yes,' said Joanna in a whisper.

'Are you sick?'

'No. But I — can you tell me where — Mr. Strange was taken?'

'Sure . . . ' the clerk gave Joanna the name of a big general hospital in the city.

'Do they know — who shot him . . . ?'

'No. It was done so quickly. Nobody

261

saw. The commissionaire was down the street, finding an automobile and by the time he'd run back to where the stranger was lying, the chap who'd gunned him had disappeared.'

'I see,' said Joanna.

'You wanting a room again?' asked the clerk.

'No,' said Joanna.

But she thought of Richard, lying outside on the pavement with the lifeblood welling from him. Richard with eyes staring, open, perhaps dead. A dark mist blotted out this frightful vision. Then Joanna toppled over. The suitcase crashed beside her.

When she opened her eyes again she found herself lying on a bed in one of the hotel bedrooms. A doctor, hastily sent for, was bending over her, holding her wrist; a finger to her pulse. She heard his voice as from miles away:

'She's coming round now . . . '

Joanna saw the doctor and a woman, one of the clerks in the hotel, beside him. She sat up. Her heart began to pound. The blood rushed to her cheeks.

'Richard . . . ' she whispered.

'Feeling better now?' said the doctor.

'Yes,' said Joanna. 'Yes. I — must go . . . to the hospital at once . . . '

'What hospital?' asked the man.

'She means she wants to see that young Englishman who has been staying here and was shot outside the hotel this afternoon,' said the woman, sotto-voce. 'She seems to be a friend of his.'

'Was someone shot?' began the doctor curiously.

'I must get up — at once — please,' Joanna broke in feverishly. She didn't want to sit here on the bed listening to these two discuss Richard's death. She wanted to get to him. To make sure that she had been told the truth. Perhaps he was not dead. Nobody seemed to know. But she must go to the hospital and find out — at once!

By the time she got away from the doctor; paid his fee; escaped the curious

263

questioning of the hotel proprietor; reached the hospital to which Richard Strange had been taken, it was nearly ten o'clock. She realised the extreme lateness of the hour. Of course by this time Richard would be dead. She would never speak to him again . . . never see him alive again.

Later she found herself in the waiting room inside the big, busy city hospital. It reeked of disinfectants. It seemed to her a place of pain, of death. She tried to steady her nerves. She could barely question the hospital nurse who came to interview her. But somehow she managed to tell the woman why she had come.

'Mr. Richard Strange . . . shot outside the Southland Hotel today . . . oh, yes, he is here,' said the nurse, having gathered what Joanna wanted, and thinking, with some pity, how ill the poor little thing looked.

'Is he — dead?' Joanna asked.

'No — but he is still unconscious,' said the nurse.

The first glimmer of light showed in Joanna's horizon. Richard wasn't dead. Thank God for that. He wasn't dead.

'How bad is he?' she asked.

'Oh, not doing too badly,' said the nurse. 'It's his shoulder. They extracted the bullet successfully. The trouble at the moment is his head. When he fell, he apparently rolled down the steps of the hotel and struck his head on the pavement. He has concussion.'

Joanna put a hand to her throat. She felt sick.

'I see. But he will — recover.'

'Yes. We hope so.'

'May I see him?'

'Are you his wife by any chance?'

'No . . . ' the colour flamed into Joanna's white face. 'Only a — very great friend.'

'Nobody may see him except his wife, I'm sorry,' said the nurse. 'Mrs. Strange has been sent for. We found letters in his pocket with his wife's name and address. We telephoned to the nursing home where Mrs. Strange has been laid up and she said she was well enough to get up and come to him. We expect her shortly. We've been so busy in the Casualty this afternoon — we had no time to sort out papers and find Mr. Strange's relations earlier . . . '

The woman rambled on . . . well-meaning, communicative. Joanna barely heard. Only one thing was clear to her. Madge had been sent for and only Madge was allowed to see Richard. His wife. His wife who had always been between them and was between them now, in this hour of crisis. Richard was very ill. When he recovered consciousness he would want her, his Anna. Not Madge who was going to divorce him. Madge had an American doctor in love with her. Why should she want her husband now? Why trouble to go to him?

A feeling of the most intense resentment against life seized Joanna in this moment. Must she always stand back and see Richard taken from her?

'I must see him, nurse, I must,' she said in a choked voice.

'I'm sorry. Only his wife may visit him tonight,' said the nurse rather coldly.

Joanna walked out of the hospital. Her whole body ached . . . her whole heart ached. She felt as though one great pain throbbed through her. For a moment she stood on the steps of the great hospital. The stars glittered overhead. In the street below, the traffic hummed and surged. San Francisco teemed with life. Life which went on . . . noisily; joyously . . . while others suffered as she was suffering now.

A woman, wrapped in handsome furs, leaning on a stick, stepped out of a private car and walked slowly up those steps. In the starlight Joanna saw her face . . . a hard, cold face framed in fair coils of hair. Joanna at once recognised her. Madge Strange. Madge had come to see Richard.

Richard's wife saw Joanna Grey and recognised her. Madge had come to see

Richard because she knew it was what the world expected from her, not because she cared whether he lived or died.

Arrangements for their divorce were in progress. She was going to marry her American doctor, and so far as Madge was capable of loving she loved him. But her dislike of Joanna, the jealousy which had taken root out in the Yukon in those days when Joanna's courage and spirit had put her so much to shame, still existed; came to the fore in this hour, showed in the maliciousness of her smile when she passed in front of Joanna.

'So you're still rushing round after my husband, Miss Grey?' she said.

'Mrs. Strange . . . Richard told me . . . he is expecting to be free . . . ' Joanna choked over the words.

'Expecting . . . but not yet free,' said Madge. 'He is still my husband. And perhaps it would be more — er — delicate if you would keep away from the hospital.'

Joanna stared at her in a stupefied way.

'But you are being divorced aren't you?'

'I really haven't made up my mind,' Madge said for sheer wanton pleasure of hurting the girl. 'We may yet make it up. Please give us the chance to make it up, anyhow, and stay away.'

Joanna's world seemed to crash at her feet. Madge Strange passed on, chuckling. She was curious to see Richard, to find out who had shot him and why.

Joanna went back to the Southland Hotel. She remembered, vaguely, that she had got enough money out of Conrad earlier in the day, to pay for her room at the hotel for some weeks. She decided to stay here tonight, stay until she could hear from the hospital that Richard was out of danger. That was all she wanted to know, before she went away. She would go away alone. She would not go back to the North, back to the eternal snows. She would try to find some sort of work here.

Madge's words had been a shock. She had been so sure that Richard was free to love her and that their love would do no harm to anybody now. But Madge had changed her mind. She wanted to keep Richard now.

Joanna wondered how much more grief and pain she would have to endure — how many more disappointments. The night passed. She slept well because she was exhausted — a drugged sleep. In the morning she dragged herself up to prepare for another wretched day. What else was there to expect now? Richard was ill. Madge might yet refuse to divorce him. Conrad Owen was somewhere in this very city hiding from the law. She was absolutely alone. Unbearably alone.

When she was sitting alone at her table in the restaurant, attempting to eat breakfast, the manager of the hotel approached her:

'Say, you are wanted in the office a moment.'

'I am — why?' asked Joanna nervously.

'A police-officer,' said the manager. He was a hard matter-of-fact man who had seen much of life and had little pity left for anybody in it except himself. 'About that husband of yours — Mr. Owen.'

Joanna put a hand to her throat. She stood up.

'My — my husband?' she stammered.

'I guess the officer will explain,' said the man none too pleasantly. 'It's a nasty business . . . to happen outside my hotel, too . . . '

A moment later Joanna was in the office and a policeman in plain clothes was telling her what had happened.

Last night Conrad Owen had hidden himself in the Chinese quarter of San Francisco. He had been embroiled in a row in some underground dope-den. His furious temper had proved his undoing for the second time within twenty-four hours. A Chinaman had annoyed him and he shot him. For that,

Conrad Owen received a knife in his throat, thrown skilfully by one of the dead man's yellow friends.

Conrad Owen died as he had lived . . . brutally and violently. He lived only long enough to confess to the crime committed outside the Southland Hotel earlier in the day and to ask that the documents in his pocket relating to the fortune of Joanna Grey should be sent to the lady who would, he said, most probably be found at the Southland under the name of Mrs. Owen. He also sent a dying message to Joanna to the effect that she was not his wife; that the man, Parson Pete, who had performed that ceremony in the Yukon was not entitled to perform a marriage ceremony.

Joanna was, comparatively, calm when she digested this information given her by the police officials. She felt that nothing could surprise her now. It was difficult to realise the news about her grandfather's fortune. That was strange — like a fairytale to wake up and find herself rich; independent; free of Conrad for ever.

But long after the police had gone and she had had time to get used to the new situation, the old sensation of hopeless grief and pain returned.

She was free. She was even rich. But Richard was not yet free. His wife was still dividing them. What use her independence, her freedom, her money? What use anything . . . without Richard?

She telephoned to the hospital and made inquiries about Richard. Her name was asked. She gave it as Joanna Grey. Never, never again need she use that hateful title 'Mrs. Owen'. She was not, she never had been, Conrad's wife. She was told to hold the line. She waited a long time. Then another voice spoke to her . . . the voice of a woman nurse.

'You say your name is Miss Grey?'

'Yes,' said Joanna.

'Are you by any chance called 'Anna'?'

'Yes,' she said and her heart missed a beat.

'Then I wonder if you would come at once,' said the nurse. 'Mr. Strange recovered consciousness at dawn and has asked frequently for somebody he calls 'Anna'. He is very ill and we think it may quieten him down if you will come and speak to him.'

Joanna swallowed hard.

'I'll come,' she said in a choked voice. 'At once.'

Richard wanted her. Called for her. What else mattered in the wide world? She must go to him.

18

Richard lay in a narrow white bed in the Men's Casualty Ward of a big San Francisco Hospital. He was surrounded by screens. He lay very still, very white . . . a bandage round his head, and one pyjama sleeve hanging loose pinned up from the wounded shoulder.

Beside him sat Joanna motionless, her hand in his. He was asleep. Ever since she had come to him, he had been asleep. When she had first entered the ward, Richard had been tossing, raving in delirium . . . calling without ceasing for his Anna. And one touch from her hand, from her lips, one whispered word: 'Richard' — and he had grown quiet.

The doctors and nurses were agreed that Miss Grey's coming had helped to save the life of the English 'casualty'. All the more interesting because he had been the victim of attempted murder and the dark-eyed beautiful girl was not his wife.

His wife had done no good at all, she had only increased the trouble when she had sat at her husband's side. She had been asked to leave which Madge had done speedily; thankful to get away.

For a solid hour, Richard Strange slept, his nervous brown fingers locked in Joanna's hand. He neither spoke nor moved. Only once his eyes opened and looked up at her. He seemed to recognise the beloved little face bending over him. For he smiled and slept again.

When he awoke he was able to speak normally and Joanna knew that the crisis was over. The tears rained down her face. She slid on her knees by the bed and put her cropped curly head against his hand. She kissed it again and again.

'Richard . . . darling . . . my darling . . .'

'Anna,' he said weakly. 'Sweetheart!'

'You're all right now,' she said.

'Absolutely. Damned silly of me to behave like this and let you down

. . . waiting for me at the station. God, what happened? Am I ill? What's wrong with my shoulder?'

She said:

'Conrad shot you, Richard.'

His eyes narrowed. He nodded once or twice.

'Ah . . . so that's it. Yes, I remember now . . . seeing him get out of that car and come toward me . . . '

'Don't — don't remember,' she said, shuddering. 'Richard — he's dead.'

'Dead! But how . . . when?'

She told him. He listened, watching her, holding on to her fingers. When she had finished, he drew her hand to his lips and kept it there for a long moment in silence. She watched him, agony in her heart and in her eyes. They loved each other so terribly, and Madge Strange was still between them.

Richard said:

'My dear . . . little Anna . . . don't worry. I shall soon get well and then we can carry on . . . pick up the thread where it snapped. This foolish wound will heal and we'll go away and forget all the horrors. Thank God you're rid of Owen! Anna don't look so sad. It's all going to come right.'

She hadn't the heart to disillusion him, to tell him what Madge had said. He was still so weak, so much in need of her love. She bent down and kissed him on the lips.

He kissed her back with the look in his eyes of a man who sees heaven.

'Now I am well again,' he whispered. 'I am well, little Anna.'

She sighed deeply, she did not speak, but she thought of the passionate hours in the deserted cabin in the White Wilderness, and of the enduring flame of their love and longing, the bitterness of unforgettable days and nights together.

She went back to the hotel and wondered how soon Madge would go to him, tell him that she intended to remain with him and to prevent him from getting his freedom.

When she was alone in the hotel, she remembered that she had not told

Richard about her inheritance. She had not thought about her grandfather's money and the property she could claim as soon as she reached England. She had thought only of Richard and his accident.

How little the money mattered. How empty a pleasure it would be to journey to her father's country — her country — as an heiress and have as much money to spend as she wanted and know she could buy whatever she wanted.

She wanted nothing. She had been used to so little in the Klondyke. She knew she would not know how to spend the money when she had it. She was not like these city girls who thronged the streets of 'Frisco; whom she saw floating about the hotel. Smart, cultured women who knew how to wear lovely clothes; who had their hair waved; their nails manicured; who drove expensive cars and enjoyed the artificial existence to which they had been educated.

'I have had no education,' Joanna

told herself when she sat in the lounge after her lonely dinner. 'I shall never like hotels and dances and restaurants. I think I'm like the wild creatures out in the Yukon. How scared they'd be in San Francisco.'

And she looked at her brown, boyish fingers which had done so much rough work and felt awkward and ill-at-ease in her blue silk dress. She thought, wistfully, of her fur coat and breeches and cap. And she thought that it would be spring up there round Fort Yukon. The snows would be melting. The waterway would thaw and ripple in a shining river through the Klondyke to Nome, leading to the sea. The spruce-forest which had been stark and grim when she had last seen it would be full of stirring life and colour again; trees breaking into green buds and flowers pushing their way through the brown earth as it softened under the sun.

Oh, those springs, those summers in the Yukon! So brief, yet so beautiful; all the more beautiful after the heartbreaking rigorous winters. As a little girl, Joanna had loved the spring and the summer; grown up year by year; familiar with the ways of bird and beast and flower. And Nature, if it was cruel at times, was not so cruel as man; as civilisation.

Joanna sat in this hotel tonight and hated men and the cities which bred them. Hated the laws of the civilised world. The kind of futile, wretched laws that divided her from Richard. She wished passionately that she could go to him in spite of Madge and divorce-laws and everything else.

She felt she would rather return to her old home and face the wild loneliness of the North than stay here or go to England to claim her fortune. Yet she knew she must go to England, because Daddy would have wished it; wanted her to see his old home and abide there in his Country.

In the morning she went again to the hospital. She found Richard stronger and better after a good night's rest. He had a gay smile and word for her when she came into the ward.

'Anna,' he said. 'Dear little Anna!'

She looked like a child in a flowered voile dress with black velvet ribbons at the throat and the short sleeves; and a black straw hat on her dark curls. Yet she seemed all of a sudden to have grown up — matured. She was a grave young woman without laughter or light in her eyes when she came and stood beside his bed.

He held out his hand.

'No smile? What is it, Anna? You're not worrying about me. This silly arm . . .' he laughed down at the empty pyjama sleeve pinned across his chest 'The doc says it's healing beautifully and my temperature's normal. I'll be out of hospital and back in the hotel in a week. Why so sad, sweetheart?'

She clung to his fingers a moment. The faintest smile curved her lips. Then she said, tremulously:

'I — Richard — your wife — '

'My wife, my dear, is busy with her lawyers divorcing me.'

'Richard, but I met her, on the steps of the hospital and she said — '

'What?'

'She might not divorce you, after all.'

Richard's face darkened.

'So that's what's worrrying you and making you look so depressed. Isn't that typical of Madge and her spiteful sort of nature. What a queer, warped nature it is, good lord! She knew perfectly well she would worry you into fits.'

'Then — is she divorcing you?'

'Yes, Anna.'

The burning colour came into her cheeks. She looked at him with almost passionate appeal in her eyes.

'Certain, Richard?'

'Read this, dear. It came this morning.'

She took the letter he gave her. A short note, typical of the writer:

'My dear Richard,
    I've decided to put through the

divorce. My solicitor here says it can be managed quickly and easily. I shall marry Boyd when it's all over and I daresay you'll be a fool and marry that little savage. I wish you joy of her. Goodbye. We shan't meet again.

Madge.'

Joanna's breath came quickly. She handed back the letter. Richard took it. He looked up at her. His eyes looked very blue, and a little whimsical.

'Are you going to let me 'be a fool' as Madge puts it and marry you, little savage?' he said.

She knelt down by the bed, thankful that the nurse had kindly put a screen about them. She caught Richard's hand and laid her cheek against it; a cheek wet with hot tears.

'I want nothing on earth but to be with you, Richard,' she said. 'But — is Mrs. Strange right? Will you — be a fool to marry me? I *am* a savage. I lack all her culture and — '

'Thank God, my dear, and all her

superiority and conceit and selfishness which have driven me mad for years,' he finished for her. He took off her hat, bent his head and touched her curls with his lips.

'Anna, my little brave one, will you make me happier than I've ever been in my life? When this thing is through, will you marry me?'

She kept her face hidden against his hand. She was crying.

'Yes, Richard.'

'Are you crying, my darling?'

'Yes. I — it's too much happiness, I can hardly bear it.'

'Anna, I never picture you crying. In my mind I see you always, fighting as gallantly as a little soldier with your back to the wall. I see you with a rifle, standing over my foolish body, keeping off the wolves, with that tight set of the bravest mouth in the world, and that light of determination in the bravest eyes. There isn't a woman on God's earth to touch you, Anna. I'm not worthy to marry you, but if you'll have me — '

'Oh, don't,' she said brokenly. 'No more . . .'

'Sit on my bed, beloved, and put your arms around me because I can't put both mine round you.'

She obeyed. Dumbly she put her arms about his neck. He put his uninjured arm around her shoulders.

'Kiss me, Anna,' he said, and closed his eyes.

She closed hers and laid her lips upon his mouth and her passionate, tormented young heart was at rest.

19

Something — Joanna scarcely knew what — kept her from telling Richard about the fortune she had inherited from her grandfather until after his divorce with Madge had been granted and the decree made absolute. Perhaps she was afraid that he might think he ought not to marry her, until she had been to England and claimed her possessions. Perhaps because possessions and the money, so far as she was concerned, meant nothing. Nothing meant anything — except Richard and his love. He was like a god to her. Her very religion. The thing for which she existed and which filled her life.

But during those months of waiting, when they had to be apart; when they could only write to each other, see each other occasionally; curb their most natural desire to be together; Joanna commenced a process of education.

She left Richard in 'Frisco and went to New York. She wanted to attend a daily college; to learn things which would befit her to be Richard's wife. Although he said he loved her as 'the little savage', she wanted to be something else; something better — for his sake.

Without telling Richard, she wrote to her grandfather's solicitors in London, sending them proofs of her identity and telling them that she would be going to England to settle up the estate, next year. Meanwhile, could they send her some money. The money came, after some delay. Joanna put most of it by and used only what was necessary for her college fees in New York.

Richard wrote to her from California:

'Don't become a fine lady, little Anna. I shan't be able to bear it if you come back to me with airs and graces.'

She wrote back:

'My beloved Richard, nothing will ever make a fine lady of me, nor shall I ever achieve airs and graces, but I must learn to write the King's English correctly; to dress decently; to manage a civilised home. But no amount of learning will stop me from loving you. I want you terribly, Richard.'

Back came a letter by return of post.

'I want you intolerably, my Anna. I can hardly stand this separation. Have you enough money? Is your father's cash lasting out? For lord's sake let me know . . .'

And one of England's richest heiresses, with a guilty little feeling in her heart, replied:
'I have enough money so far. I adore you.'
Then the exile in New York came to an end; the college-trained young lady departed for California, and Richard

Strange, divorced from his wife and free to marry again, met her at the other end of the Eerie line in mingled ecstasy and fear.

When she stepped out of the train he was waiting for her, looking years younger, brown, fit and gayer. He gave one look at her; rather a smart Joanna in a well-cut suit and American shirt-waist and wine-coloured tie; a chic little hat on her cropped head. Hungrily Richard seized her hands.

'Anna. Have you altered? Oh, lord, you look so smart. I knew you would become — '

But he said no more. The chic hat came off; the black curls, still boyishly short, were rumpled; and a small, quivering figure hurled itself into his arms, in front of the crowds on the platform. An ardent little face was raised to his; an intense voice said:

'I haven't changed. Richard, I haven't changed. Hold me. Kiss me.'

Then he knew it was the same Joanna. And he said, 'Oh, thank God, my little Anna,' and kissed her.

The honeymoon chosen by Joanna and Richard after their marriage in a San Francisco registry office, would have appeared to most people extraordinary. It was not spent in Honolulu; or Tahiti or any romantic, favourite island of sunshine and flowers. But up in the white, severe isolation of the Klondyke; in the bitter, strenuous North where most men live and die for gold.

Joanna and Richard went there for love and for sentiment and for the sake of the past.

Up there, they had first met and loved and suffered. They wanted to go back and be happy there, together. And Joanna had another reason. She wanted to find Kiche again; to reward the faithful Indian for his many services to her and her father.

She found him still at Fort Yukon. The Indian, delighted to see his little white lady again, accompanied her and her husband to John Grey's old cabin. And there, although it was mid-winter;

the hardest time in the Klondyke, Joanna and Richard spent a strangely beautiful week.

On the first night of their arrival Joanna refused to depart from any of her old habits and customs. She changed her travelling suit for an old dress, fur coat, breeches and cap. She lit her oil-lamp and her stove. She cooked the supper. She washed up. She made Richard sit in John Grey's old rocking-chair and smoke his pipe. And then, when the labours were over, she curled on the floor at his feet with her head against his knee and was utterly content.

'Richard,' she said. 'Do you know that this is heaven?'

'Yes, Anna,' he said, stroking her curls. 'And you are the small angel that makes it so.'

She laughed and sighed again. Through the square pane window she could see stars glittering, a wilderness of ice and snow and the frowning spruce-forest. And in the silence, she heard the old, familiar hunger-cry of a wolf. But she did not care. To be in here in warmth, in such happiness with Richard as his wife was a thing almost too good to be true.

He leaned down and pulled her up on to his knees.

'Why so thoughtful, my Anna?'

'I'm remembering something.'

'What, beloved?'

'Lovely things about you when I first met you. How you hated being shut up in that other shanty with me and snapped and frowned at me.'

'That wasn't very lovely. I was bitter about women and life. You must forgive me, my dear.'

'I don't want to forgive it. I like to cherish the memory of it. It's lovely because you don't snap or frown at me now.'

'I might at any moment,' said Richard, and hugged her.

She leaned her head back on his shoulder and closed her eyes.

'It's awfully nice being your wife, Richard.'

'Are you really happy, Anna?'

'So happy, I could die.'

'You're such a generous lover, sweet-heart. You don't know what a lot that means. It only makes me realise more profoundly what an empty life I used to lead with *her*.'

Joanna's eyes opened and looked at him gravely.

'I hope we shall have a baby,' she said, and said it so simply that the man could only hold her closer and kiss her with wordless passion.

'I think somehow we will,' she added. 'It would be lovely — to be the mother of your son.'

'That will be another dream come true, my Anna.'

Silence a moment. He rocked gently in the old chair with her in his arms. Then, suddenly, she said:

'Richard, I've got a confession to make.'

'Make away, then, sweetheart.'

'We've got to go to England one day soon.'

'We will, of course. But what's the confession?'

'I'm afraid I've got a lot of money. What shall we do with it?'

He stopped rocking and looked down at her.

'Anna, you've got a lot of money? How?'

She told him. He listened with a grave face. Then he said:

'Anna, what a secret to keep locked up all this time. Why didn't you tell me before?'

'Because I was afraid you might ... refuse to marry me ... or something stupid.' She put her arms about his neck and laid a warm, flushed cheek against his. 'Darling, darling Richard, don't be cross. You said you might frown at any moment, but I couldn't bear it.'

'Oh, my dearest,' he said, and kissed her until she was breathless. 'As if I could be cross. But it's a bit of a shock to find I've married an heiress.'

'It needn't make any difference.'

'All right, it shan't.'

He stood up, and picked her right up in his arms. He stooped and blew out the little oil-lamp. The moonlight and firelight fell upon her face, making it strangely lovely.

'What are you going to do, Richard?' she asked in a small voice.

'Treat you as though neither of us had a bean. Only rich people stay up late and burn their oil. We're poor and we're going to turn in. See, Anna Strange?'

She laughed and snuggled deeper in his arms. He carried the little fur-clad figure through the door to their room. In the kitchen Kiche made up the fire for the night. And from the distance came another sad, fierce hunger-cry from a lone wolf.

But even if they heard it, nobody in John Grey's cabin seemed to care.

We do hope that you have enjoyed reading this large print book.

Did you know that all of our titles are available for purchase?

We publish a wide range of high quality large print books including:
Romances, Mysteries, Classics
General Fiction
Non Fiction and Westerns

Special interest titles available in large print are:
The Little Oxford Dictionary
Music Book, Song Book
Hymn Book, Service Book

Also available from us courtesy of Oxford University Press:
Young Readers' Dictionary
(large print edition)
Young Readers' Thesaurus
(large print edition)

For further information or a free brochure, please contact us at:
Ulverscroft Large Print Books Ltd.,
The Green, Bradgate Road, Anstey,
Leicester, LE7 7FU, England.
Tel: (00 44) 0116 236 4325
Fax: (00 44) 0116 234 0205